# Also By Christie Ridgway

## 7-Stud Club
All In (#1)
No Limits (#2)
Ante Up (#3), *Comng Soon!*

## Heartbreak Hotel
Our Last First Kiss (#1)
Me and Mr. Jones (#2)
My Quickie Wedding (#3)
We Belong Together (#4), *Coming soon!*

## Almost
Almost Wonderful (#1)
Almost Always (#2)
Almost Everything (#3)
Almost Paradise (#4)

## Rock Royalty Series
Light My Fire (#1)
Love Her Madly (#2)
Break on Through (#3)
Touch Me (#4)
Wishful Sinful (#5)
Wild Child (#6)
Who Do You Love (# 7)
Love Me Two Times (#8)

## Billionaire's Beach Series
Take Me Tender (#1)
Take Me Forever (#2)
Take Me Home (#3)
The Scandal (#4)
The Seduction (#5)
The Secret (#6)

## In Hot Water Duo
First Comes Love (#1) and Then Comes Marriage (#2)

## Holiday Duet
Must Love Mistletoe (#1) amd Not Another New Year's (#2)

## Standalone Novels
Nothing But Blue Skies
Out on a Limb (A Novella)
Snow Job
The Thrill of It All
Three Little Words

*Thanks to all my wonderful readers!*

# NO LIMIT

*7-Stud Club, Book 2*

# CHRISTIE RIDGWAY

Printed in the United States of America

ISBN: 978-1-939286-49-9

# Chapter 1

The evening of card play over, Eli King walked the last of his poker buddies, Maddox Kelly, toward his home's large foyer. Six feet from the front door, they halted, staring at the obstacle directly ahead. On a floral hooked rug—handcrafted by the second oldest of Eli's four younger sisters, a fine arts major—sat a jumbled mass of duffels, wheeled suitcases, toiletry kits, and shopping bags filled to the brim with who-knew-what.

Maddox slanted him a glance. "Is it like mold? I swear that pile grew in the four hours since I walked in and managed—with my superior skill—to win sixty smackers off you."

"Welcome to life with a household of women," Eli muttered, carefully skirting a sloppy heap of scarves and hats so he could reach the worn brass knob. The porch light shone through the lace covering the windowed half of the door, a curtain Sister #2 had sewn during her seamstress phase. "And I lost that final hand because I was distracted by your last girlfriend. She texted to lament your repulsive, troll-like features."

They grinned at each other as Eli drew open the door, letting in the chill of a mid-April night in Sawyer Beach, a central California coastal town. Maddox sauntered over the threshold then paused to look back. "What are you going to do with yourself when all four of them head out on that road trip tomorrow?"

Eli barely resisted rubbing his palms together in gleeful anticipation. "Two weeks without needing to herd four females with four distinct minds of their own? I've been planning my time since last spring break."

"Do tell."

"Engaging in bachelor behaviors that any other normal, red-blooded twenty-nine-year-old man enjoys."

"Ah." Maddox said, nodding. "Eating Slim Jim sticks for breakfast and pawing through the pile of dirty laundry to find a pair of socks that might possibly pass the smell test?"

Eli's lip curled. "It must suck to be you. I'm talking about some social life, Mad. Late nights. Even staying up, maybe, to greet the dawn."

"Greet the dawn," his friend repeated, smirking. His forefinger shot out to point at Eli, center-mass. "You're talking about sex. It's been a long dry spell, huh?"

As if he'd admit it. Though it was over 300 days since he'd shared sheets with a woman, not that he was counting. "Look, I'm only willing to say that I have some ideas about how to fill my after-work hours." Getting away from the nursery business in the spring season was a no-go, he'd discovered. Last year, he'd gone on a guys' trip for ten days and returned to a surfeit of staffing and supply snafus.

"Well, you have my number if you need bail, condoms, or advice," Maddox said, "though I hope not in that order."

Having a good friend employed by the local police department wasn't something to joke about. "Yeah, thanks."

With a final wave, Maddox headed into the night, leaving Eli to yank out his phone for a quick check of the time. Nearly eleven p.m., and four sisters not yet tucked into bed. They must have added to the mountain of belongings on their way out for the evening, while he was deep in poker play with the six friends that had gathered together for a weekly game since their stint in high school Auto Shop.

In the dining room, he collected the bags of non-greasy snacks left on the sideboard and walked them into the kitchen. It was a large space, with lots of counters and cabinets, a farmhouse sink, and a built-in bench along with table and chairs for seating. His buddy Hart Sawyer, who led a construction business, told him he should knock out a couple of walls to modernize the place, but Eli was leaving that to the next owner.

As soon as the sixteen-year-old twins, Lynnie and Molly, left for college, he had the approval of the four girls to sell the family homestead. They'd all been there since their births, not moving even when their parents died in a car accident eleven years before. But his sisters claimed not to possess a sentimental attachment and the place was going to be too big for just one bachelor bent on claiming a single life. A single life put on hold since he took over for Mom and Dad as head of the King household.

The dishwasher was on its last legs, but Eli optimistically filled it with glassware and the utensils and bowls they'd used to eat his famous chili. The host of poker night provided dinner and drinks for the crowd while the crowd contributed during-play edibles that wouldn't leave a stain on the cards. Somebody had brought gummy bears—most likely Boone, because he had a soft spot for Eli's sisters and would have purchased their favorite—so Eli rolled down the top of the bag and secured it with a rubber band then tossed it onto the kitchen table. Tomorrow he'd tuck it into the center console of Nora's small SUV, the car they were taking on their drive to Seattle.

The gummies slid across the surface of the table and fell to the floor, so he crossed to the bag with a grimace and swooped down for retrieval. He set the candy beside the map he'd picked up at the auto club—he'd joined when the first of the girls, Nora, got behind the wheel and there were now four King sister memberships. "God help us all," he muttered, the same phrase he spoke aloud every time he thought of his youngest siblings driving.

For a moment he hovered over the spread-out map and traced with his finger the route they'd take up the California coast and then into Oregon and Washington. He'd starred the two places he thought would make safe and enjoyable overnights along the way, despite the rolled eyes and nonstop gripes he'd received from Nora, Allison, Lynnie, and Molly.

They could navigate themselves, they'd said. They had smartphones and cell service and a surfeit of brain matter. They didn't need his guidance.

They didn't say they didn't need him. The twins had been just shy of five, and the other two were nine and eleven when Eli had taken over the shopping and cooking and laundry. He'd been eighteen and already working near full-time at the family nursery. Instead of going away to college, he'd enrolled in classes at the local community college.

But quickly lectures and readings had gone out the window for him and the only homework he'd become dedicated to was the homework assigned to his sisters. Sure, at times it had felt like a burden, but he'd never considered the girls *themselves* a burden.

Now they were growing up and eager to try out their wings.

Meaning it was his turn to fly.

Full flight wasn't for another year-plus, when Lynnie and Molly moved into dorms, but he was going to take a practice run these next two weeks. Smiling at his own eagerness, he folded the map and set the gummy bears on top of it. The feeling was a little like Christmas Eve, he realized, during those years when his folks were alive, before it was he who was staying up all night wrapping presents, assembling toys, and scarfing down the treats left out for Santa.

The squeal and bang of the front door opening and shutting snagged his attention. Footsteps sounded, some tramping up the stairs, another quick set heading for him and the kitchen.

Molly swung through the entry from the hallway,

her cheeks flushed and small wisps of hair escaping the long French braid hanging over one shoulder. He'd taught himself how to achieve that style through internet how-to videos years ago. Now the girls could manage it themselves or had a sister or friend attend to the task.

He didn't miss it, he told himself.

"Bro," Molly said by way of greeting, heading for the refrigerator.

"Sis," he replied, smiling at her back. He didn't have favorites, but Mol was the one who invariably checked in with him whenever she got home.

"Did you win tonight?" his youngest sister asked, sliding out a colander of washed grapes and plucking a few of the green fruit free.

"Of course," he lied. A big brother had a rep to maintain.

She sent him a suspicious glance over her shoulder. But he had practice at this, too. The kid had believed in the tooth fairy way beyond the ordinary use-by date.

Pulling out his phone, he tapped to his notes app. "Who came in with you?"

Molly turned, gave him an eye roll that he was also long familiar with. "Dude," she said, in a censuring tone.

"What?"

"Please." She shook her head. "Tell me you're not checking us off like you usually do."

"What part of 'like I usually do' doesn't compute?"

"That stupid list you make every time we walk out the door is annoying," Molly declared, in the tone of aggrieved teenagers everywhere. "And then when you make a mark once we get back home…well, that's so Captain von Trapp."

It wasn't like he could miss a *Sound of Music* reference, since it had been his littlest sister's favorite movie from ages four to ten. "You know, that's sparked a good idea," he said. "I could assign you each your own whistle. When you come in, you just make the sound and I'll hear it from wherever I am in the house, check you off that way."

Molly sighed, as he'd expected. Then she laughed, which he'd also expected. "You're weird."

"The goal of all big brothers everywhere," he said. "Add overprotective and I'll sleep like a baby."

"Make that really weird," Molly replied, and returned the colander to the refrigerator. "I'm going upstairs now. And before you ask, all four of us came in together."

"Great." Eli didn't bother trying to hide the fact that he registered each girl's return on his phone. "Have a good rest," he said, as she approached to kiss his cheek good night.

"We're off early in the morning," Molly reminded him. "I'd say you don't have to get up to see us go, but why waste my breath?"

He grinned. "Yes, why?" And laughed as that got him the trifecta—rolled eyes, shaking head, and gusty sigh. As he turned off the kitchen light, he listened to her clamber up the stairs, and then began walking through the first floor to flip other switches and double-check the locks.

At last, he stood in the foyer again, frowning at the pile, which seemed to have grown another two feet in all directions. Where did all that stuff come from? The oldest two had apartments at college and surely they'd left at least some of their belongings there.

Ah, well. If they'd have a better spring break dragging everything they owned along with them, what did he care? It equaled, as a matter of fact, a better spring break for him.

Thinking of the personal freedom lying ahead, he cast aside his worries over his four younger siblings and their imminent adventure.

"Carpe diem," he murmured, his mood as free as he was going to be in about six hours when he waved them on their way. Carpe diem was going to be his mantra. Seize the day and enjoy the hell out of each unfettered moment. The only thing that would hold him down, he decided, would be some willing lady wanting to ride him, cowgirl-style.

Smiling at the thought, he reached to turn off the porch light. But before his fingers found the switch, a knock sounded on the door. His head snapped toward the glass and through the lace he detected the shadow of a form.

Slight form.

Female.

He frowned. Who was out in the cold at this time of night?

Instinct clamored at him. It could mean trouble, it said. Something that might dampen all this sense of pleasure-in-the-offing. *Ignore the summons.*

But instead he smothered the inner voice and did what he'd been doing for the last eleven years—Eli stepped up.

The squeal of the hinges sounded like a second warning as he swung open the front door. At the bottom of the steps stood a woman, and at the look of her his body tensed, in an instant his muscles and nerves going on high, pulsing alert. *Danger danger danger.*

Which made no sense, because she was dressed in sneakers, jeans, and a long-sleeved T-shirt with scattered bleach stains. Even now she took a couple of steps back and the landscape lighting caught on a gleaming cap of blonde curls. She looked innocent. Innocuous.

Like an angel.

Eli suppressed an acute urge to slam the door in her face.

From her position halfway between the porch and her car, Sloane Clarke stared up at the lean, muscled man framed by his front door. A wash of heat prickled across her scalp and headed southward. Not good. She took a quick health assessment, concerned she might be coming down with something.

Single mothers didn't have such a luxury.

But swallowing proved her throat felt just fine and her head wasn't hurting. No other bodily aches and pains. So, dismissing the moment, she smiled. "Hi, I'm Sloane?"

Gah. It came out with an upward inflection, a sign of insecurity leftover from her growing-up years that she'd been determined motherhood would extinguish. And it had—not since an obstetric nurse had placed infant Paige—now almost four years old—into her arms had Sloane sounded so uncertain.

Eli King, she decided, was to blame with the way he was looking at her with such grave eyes. And maybe some of the responsibility lay with the Parade of Hotties, too, the men she'd seen through her living room window drive up to his home tonight. A throng of good-looking guys weren't common in her world of toddlers and spreadsheets.

Now clearing her throat, she tried again, intending to project that, yes, she was quite certain of her very own name. "Sloane Clarke."

His head tilted, his shoulder-length hair shifting with the movement. The stuff was smooth, glossy, and actually appeared almost as long as her own, because the curl factor caused hers to shrink a couple of inches when dry. "Sloane," Eli repeated.

More feverish heat swept over her as he continued staring. She gestured vaguely behind her back, in the direction of the residence across the street. "I live over there," she said, "across the road. The small cottage? It was a carriage house, I've been told, for another larger place, long since gone. But I like it. It's enough space, really, because I don't have a lot of stuff and I enjoy it out here, it feels almost rural but still close to town." Realizing she was babbling, she forced her mouth to shut.

God, he must think she was an idiot. But then she was talking again, without the permission of her more poised self. "I like my big oak tree in front and there's a creek running through the backyard. But of course your landscaping is lovely. I appreciate it every day when I come home, the lush lawn and those hydrangea bushes are sure to be beautiful this summer. Not to mention…"

But then her brain caught up with her mouth, and the mentioning halted, midstream.

"Take a breath," he suggested kindly, a hint of a smile around his lips, revealing a glimpse of strong, white teeth. "And then tell me why you're here."

"Oh." As directed, she sucked in some air and hoped her embarrassed blush didn't turn her fair skin an unbecoming shade of red. Then she lifted the pair of rubber rain boots she carried in her left hand. "One of the twins left these at my place and I wanted to be sure to return them before the big road trip."

"Okay," he said, then pointed at her feet. "But why are you *there* there?"

He meant why had she knocked on his door then scurried off the porch like a timid rabbit. But it had nothing to do with bravery. Glancing over her shoulder, she checked on Paige, asleep in her car seat, her towhead lolling. "I want to keep an eye on my daughter," she explained. "We were at some friends earlier and were on our way home when I remembered the boots."

Eli's expression changed, from somewhat curious to...well, blank. "Ah," he said, then made his way down the stairs, his long legs eating up the distance between them.

Despite an impulse to scuttle backward again, Sloane planted her sneakers on the ground and outstretched her arm. The boots dangled in the air until he took hold of them.

Her arm dropped.

"Thank you," he said, then hesitated. "I'll put these with the other things they're bringing."

"Great." Without a real goodbye, they began to move in opposite directions. She wondered if she'd ever have a word with him again.

Her belly fluttered, peevish butterflies dodging and weaving, which she could only hope wasn't a second sign of oncoming illness. With the weekend on the horizon and the twins unavailable to babysit—

"*Wait*," Sloane said, spinning around.

Eli turned too, his foot on the lowest step. "Something else?" His expression looked wary.

"I made treats for their road trip," she said, and jogged around the front of her car to open the passenger seat. She removed the shoebox she'd lined with foil and held it toward him with two hands, like an offering.

He lowered the boots to the step and then returned her way, accepting the container. "Treats?" he asked, raising one brow.

Sloane found the gesture fascinating. And this close she could smell him too, a lime aftershave with an added hint of chili spices. Very manly. Her daughter's daddy had worn cologne, a too-sweet scent selected by his mother, "Rice Krispies treats. You can go ahead and have one if you'd like."

A strange expression crossed his face, one she couldn't interpret. Reluctance?

"Really," she said, to encourage him. "I made a lot." On another breath she was babbling again, a brook fed by some river of nervous reaction she had to the way he looked, the way he smelled, that amazing eyebrow. "They're really easy. The cereal, of course, then you melt together some butter and marshmallows—"

"I know how to make Rice Krispies treats," Eli said. "It brings back some bad memories, as a matter of fact."

"Oh, sorry." She felt her face blanch, which at least would neutralize the earlier redness. "Really sorry, but I—"

"Stop," he said, holding up a hand.

Yay. She needed some sort of chatter control mechanism and that big palm seemed to do the trick.

"The memories aren't all bad," he said, "but I had to help Allison make what seemed to be thousands one weekend a while back. They were a donation for the drama club bake sale—drama club was her thing-of-the-moment—and we made them plain, and with chocolate chips, and with butterscotch chips, and with pieces of dried fruit, and with—well, you get the idea."

She did, and it charmed her, to think of big brother Eli King committing himself to a weekend in the kitchen. Another rush of strange heat flashed over her skin and she made a mental note to take two pain relievers before bedtime.

"Then the dog took off with a plateful and rolled in them instead of eating the damn things. Next he ran his sticky self out to the yard where he took a dirt bath. Think about the cleanup involved."

She grinned at him. "Probably like washing up a toddler who's smeared herself with ice cream before vigorous play in the sandbox."

He'd started to smile too, then it died as he glanced over her shoulder toward her car. "Sloane," he said, his voice going quiet. "You should probably be getting your daughter to bed."

"You're right." Paige needed to go down in her own bed for the night and Sloane required eight hours also, to clear her muddled brain. Because sometime during the last bit of conversation, Eli King had drawn closer to her and she'd noticed, besides his delicious man-smell, the undeniable attractiveness of the sinewy, muscled length of him. Worse, for the tiniest of seconds, she'd imagined what it might be like to lean into his strength.

Which proved she had to be verging on unwell. When she'd become Paige's mom she'd vowed to never depend upon anyone but herself.

"Good night, Eli," she said, with a short nod.

"Goodbye, Sloane," he answered. They turned away from each other.

"*Wait*," a new voice called out.

Sloane's spine snapped straight and her head turned to see Molly King running down the porch steps, wearing floppy flannel pants and an oversized T-shirt. Eli looked at his sister, a puzzled expression on his face.

"Mol?" he asked.

"Perfect," she cried, "to catch you two together."

Her brother frowned. "You didn't 'catch' us at anything, Molly. Sloane brought over rain boots and Rice Krispies treats." He handed his sister the box.

"Cool," she said, tucking them under one arm. Then she tucked her other hand in her brother's elbow and towed him toward where Sloane stood, preparing to slip into the driver's seat. "I don't believe you two have formally met."

"We've been talking—"

"Sloane Clarke, Eli King. Eli King, Sloane Clarke," Molly said.

Eli's expression signaled patience stretching thin. "Okay, Mol, introductions are done and it's late. We all need to get inside to our respective homes."

"As soon as I tell Sloane that we're counting on her."

"Um, what?" Sloane asked.

"She lives right across the street," the girl said, addressing her brother.

"I got that."

Molly turned to Sloane. "It won't be any inconvenience at all," she declared. "But we'll feel better for it, all four of us."

Eli sucked in a long breath. "Mol, what are you talking about?"

She wagged her finger at him. "Don't think we don't know about your plans for the next two weeks, Elijah Henry King."

In the light glowing from the windows and the outdoor fixtures set strategically around the King front yard, Sloane could see a flag of color splashing each of Eli's cheekbones. *Hmm.*

She rocked back on her heels, allowing herself a moment to enjoy his discomfiture. Did that make her a bad person? "What are these plans of your brother's you're talking about, Molly?" she asked.

Eli shot her a quick glance and she barely managed to suppress her smirk. Handsome, sexy man, home alone without the constricting presence of four younger sisters, two of them teenagers? It didn't take a leap of understanding to figure he was planning on turning the family home into a temporary den of iniquity. She smiled at him, sweetness and light. "Or maybe I should be asking you, Eli. Should I be worried about witnessing—"

"Nothing like you're imagining," Eli said abruptly, his brows slamming together.

He feared her speculating in front of his little sister, which made Sloane want to laugh. "I only intended to ask if you were planning on hosting poker nights past eleven," she said innocently.

His disgruntled look made her swallow another giggle. When was the last time she'd had this much fun?

"You know about poker night?" he asked.

"It's not poker night we sisters are worried about," Molly said, so Sloane didn't have to explain how she'd soaked up any and every detail the King sisters dropped about their brother. "It's whether…" The girl sent Eli a significant look.

He tensed. "Whether what?"

"Whether you're going to take proper care of yourself while we're gone," Molly answered. "It can't be all pizza all the time, Eli. And showers. You mustn't forget showers."

His expression signaled outrage. "When haven't I showered?" he demanded.

"We don't want you to begin a bad habit," Molly explained. She put the box of treats on the top of Sloane's car so she could jam her fists on her hips. "Let's talk about shaving. That you've been known to forget, admit it. But you have to remember to use your razor at least every other day, otherwise you scare off the customers at the nursery. Can you promise to do that?"

"No," Eli said, clearly unwilling to take orders from his little sister.

"I thought so." Molly sighed. "That's why Sloane's going to promise to keep tabs on you."

"Huh?" Sloane looked at the girl. "What?"

"Once a day. Twice would be better, if you can manage it. Just show up at the door, give him a holler, and make sure he's doing the right things."

Eli was glaring at his sister, clearly murder on his mind. Sloane had to swallow more laughter. The man obviously wasn't interested in having a comportment monitor sicced on him.

"Sure, Molly," she said, managing to keep a straight face. "I'd be happy to keep tabs on your big brother's behavior." Glancing at Eli, she could see he didn't find anything about this even remotely humorous, which only tickled her funny bone more.

"Really," she said, addressing him now with overt enthusiasm. "It's no problem. Happy to help."

"Awesome sauce!" Molly crowed, clapping her hands. Then she grabbed one of Eli's and one of Sloane's. "Shake on it," she said, and pressed their palms together.

Rocking Sloane's world.

Her heart slammed against her ribs, then a flash bang of sensation sparked from the place they touched, shooting up her arm. Her fingers spasmed, closing over Eli's, and his did the same.

Politeness on his side? She didn't know, because she couldn't bring herself to look at him. Or breathe. After a moment she managed to yank her hand free, but she kept her eyes downcast as she rushed to slip behind the wheel. With the car started, she rolled down the window and, trying to keep up appearances, called out a faux cheery good night.

Eli didn't bother replying, but Molly smiled big. "Don't forget your promise," she called out, grabbing the Rice Krispies from the car roof.

Sloane waved, but didn't speak, the promise she'd made a tiny blip on her worry radar. Looming large was the fact that she'd figured out the cause of all her physical responses tonight—the heat, the belly flutters, the muddled state of mind. It wasn't an illness in the health sense of the word.

It was something else altogether, that went a long way to explaining all the times she'd caught herself stealing glances at Eli King since she moved into her little house four months ago. All the times she'd ferreted away the nuggets of info about the man his sisters had dropped. That reaction to the simple touch of his hand on hers confirmed it.

She had a thing for him.

A ridiculous, nonsensical, inconvenient thing.

Maybe even dangerous.

With the upcoming visit from Paige's grandparents in the offing—a visit that would take all her powers of patience and self-control—this was no time to be distracted.

Particularly not by a knee-buckling crush on the man across the street.

# Chapter 2

Eli checked the old clock mounted on the wall of his office, noting it read five o'clock. Time to go. Sure, the nursery stayed open until dusk, but he'd been chained to his office chair since six a.m., arriving after seeing off his four sisters. Thinking of them, he glanced at his phone to ensure he hadn't missed a text.

Nothing since they'd given him a snarky rundown of their lunch selections.

It was going to be more than nice to get home and start his weekend—no, *two weeks* without younger sibling-attitude in his face.

He was still staring at his phone when his assistant Marie came to stand in the doorway, wearing her work uniform of jeans and a King Nursery T-shirt. At sixty, she looked hardly a day past forty, with her gray-less hair layered around her face, a smile curving her lips and reaching to crinkle her brown eyes at the corners. "You're going to miss them. Admit it."

He took a last check of his cell, then shoved it in his back pocket. "Miss who?"

She gave him a long-suffering look, which she was thoroughly entitled to, as she'd worked for his dad and then Eli, putting up and helping him cope with the inevitable pains of taking over as boss of the family business when he was eighteen, grieving but determined. "Your sisters, of course."

Instead of answering, Eli stood and began a half-hearted attempt at straightening the papers on the battered metal desk that had been his father's, and his father's before him. Everything about the office was nearly the same as the way his dad had left it, though there were fewer wholesale catalogs cluttering the space than he remembered as a kid.

He shut down his computer. These days, most of his ordering was done online.

His gaze went to the clock again, a promotional piece from a seed company having long since left the marketplace. The yellowed plastic case and the colorful face decorated with dancing cornstalks were too familiar to replace. And hey, it still worked.

"Five," Eli said to Marie. "Time for us both to clear out. Doug's in charge of shutting down for the night." There was a caretaker who lived on the nursery's property full-time as well, so the list of closing tasks for the last staff member was a short one. "Grab your purse and make for your Friday night happy-hour meet up with your husband."

"I will. Russ said he's running a little late, though." She waved a manila folder. "I'm just reminding you of that field trip we have scheduled for next week. The liability paperwork was just now emailed from the elementary school's extended care program."

"Right." With Easter coming late this year, so was spring vacation. The program's administrator had proposed to Eli an enrichment visit for the younger kids out on break. "I modified the schedule to include a couple of extra bodies to help out that day."

"I'll make sure there's strawberries and apple juice for a snack," Marie said.

"Great idea." Eli felt for his keys. Before him lay a Friday night devoid of plans besides as many beers as he decided to consume and whatever television caught his attention. No need to set a good example by limiting his intake or opting for educational entertainment—his sisters watched enough of that reality crap, so he usually tried modeling better choices.

Jeez, he thought, in sudden realization. What a dull life he'd been leading.

"Oh," Marie said, as she swung around. "Sophie Daggett's here to see you."

Eli nearly groaned, lamenting the delay to his I'm-free Friday, but almost before that thought was completed, Sophie herself hurried in, looking more chipper than she had in the two months since Hart Sawyer's fiancée had died of an aneurism.

The tragedy had affected their entire group of friends—the poker buddies and the circle surrounding them—and Sophie's usual bounce had gone missing. But now she was smiling, and recalling the likely reason for her visit, he decided he should be smiling too.

So he did, gesturing for her to take one of his visitor chairs and dropping back into the seat behind his desk. "Soph," he said. "Looking good."

She was petite and blonde—not the same corn-silk shade of that woman from last night, the one he'd dismissed from his mind the moment she'd reversed out of his driveway. Sophie's hair was a honey blonde and she tucked it behind her ears as she sat.

"I've found you three great women," she said in a loud voice.

"*Shh!*" Jeez. He glanced over her shoulder, toward his office door. "Do you want the whole nursery to know you're playing matchmaker?"

"*I'm* not ashamed," she said. "Neither should you be. You're a busy man who's afraid to join an online dating service. How else are you going to meet people?"

His gaze darted toward the door again. "I'm not *afraid.*"

"Oh, come on, I know you shake in your boots thinking Nora or Allison might stumble across your profile."

Eli suppressed his shudder at the thought. "Do those services have a way of preventing that?" he demanded. "And if so, how trustworthy might their safeguards be?"

Sophie waved away his concern. "It doesn't matter. I volunteered and you let me take on the job. I've even arranged the dates for you. All three women are quite interested."

God, he hoped Sophie hadn't promised white lace and wedding rings. "They know I'm still raising Lynnie and Molly and—"

"They know everything," Sophie said, waving her hand again.

He decided against enquiring further. Though he

hadn't told his friend's younger sister that he was primarily looking to get laid during the next two weeks, when she'd offered to scout around for him, he'd agreed. He wasn't expecting every date to end in bed, anyway. As long as Sophie hadn't advertised him as in the market for marriage, he was willing to make a new acquaintance or two, free of naked expectations. So the three dates sounded good.

Unless…

"No single mothers, right?" he asked, adamant against such complications. "Nobody—"

"Stop fretting," Sophie said. "Like you, none of them will turn into a pumpkin or need to pay off a babysitter at midnight."

Relieved, Eli didn't hesitate to take a look at the photos on Sophie's phone. Three pretty faces and he decided meeting them would be no hardship. Clearly pleased as well, Sophie let him walk her from the building and give a grateful kiss to her cheek as goodbye. Her vehicle exited the lot as he watched, then he headed to his own and made the short drive home.

Entering his house through the garage and into the kitchen, he breathed deep. Okay, the air hadn't lost all its girly notes, but he was accustomed to the mixed fragrances of several perfumed products. At the refrigerator, he pulled out a cold one and popped the top.

Taking a sip, he walked to the foyer to retrieve the mail that had been slipped through the slot on the front door. Worthless circulars and a catalog of pricey lingerie, addressed to Lynnie. Frowning, he tossed it face down on the coffee table in the family room and dropped to the couch. Should he say something to her about it? Have another talk about boys and what they wanted?

A thought that only chafed at him as he recalled what *he* wanted for the next couple of weeks.

Shit.

He flicked on the TV remote and rolled through the channels. Nothing appealed to him. Not sports, not politics, not some explosion-heavy movie that he'd seen before.

Four thousand cable channels and he could only think how quiet the house was over the rat-a-tat-tat of an assault weapon coming from the surround speakers.

Maybe he should start a load of laundry.

Then, horrorstruck by the reflexive thought, he jumped to his feet. No red-blooded American male was going to fill up the washing machine on a Friday night. Well, he had in the past, upon discovering that the soccer uniforms or the dancewear weren't clean for Saturday morning, but the past was over, at least for the next couple of weeks.

To escape any further domestic urges, he exited the house.

Some fresh air, he decided, would clear his head and sweep away old habits which were dying much too hard. He was supposed to start livin' the life. Now. This evening.

Though the sun remained in the sky, the day was cooling down and he was glad he'd pulled on a sweatshirt. The front lawn looked a little ragged and he'd get on it first thing in the morning—unless he suffered from a hangover, in which case he'd give himself a pass until noon.

Of course, he hadn't even consumed half the beer

he'd started, but there was still plenty of time to tie one on. Swinging bachelors could do that.

All part of livin' the life.

At random, he took a right at the bottom of the drive. The road wasn't bounded by sidewalks, but a whitewashed split-rail fence delineated the King property. He ambled along it, focus straight ahead, when the tinny sounds of an old pop tune reached his ears. Something about a party.

Glancing to his left, he saw the small stucco house, shaded by a huge, gnarly-armed oak. No fence sat between the road and the yard beneath the tree's overhang that was mostly packed dirt with the occasional sprouting of ivy. Then out the open front door a girl-child danced, a pink plastic boom box clutched in her small fist. A dog, fur golden and shaggy, trotted at her heels.

Then its head came up, and with a booming *whoof*, it raced in a direct path toward Eli.

Shit. He braced for impact, maybe even bloodletting.

At the last moment, a sharp whistle caused the creature to stop in its tracks, long ears flying out. It looked toward the shrill noise. So did Eli.

There she was. Sloane Clarke. In another pair of jeans, the same sneakers, a T-shirt with *Duffy's Does It Green & Local* stretching across her ample breasts.

He wished he hadn't noticed that. He wished he hadn't seen any of her again, because he'd already spent too much time banishing the woman from his mind, where she persisted in returning to linger at its fringes. Because last night, he'd decided it was best to pretend she didn't exist.

She, however, seemed to have no such ambition

as she jogged across the dirt to the edge of the road opposite him.

Her breasts bounced as she did so, and he comforted himself by deciding that no man under eighty would have been able to not-see something like that. But as she got closer, he took control of himself and fixed his gaze on her face.

Those big, round blue eyes. That bow-shaped mouth.

*God.*

"How are you?" she asked, those lips stretching into a smile. Her teeth were small and white.

Eli had no idea why he imagined them taking a bite, right on the meatiest curve of his pec. He was a sick bastard, he decided, to have such ideas when her dog was right there.

Not to mention her kid, who was now spinning in circles to what he now recognized was a Pink tune, sung in childish voices. An old CD, he guessed. His sisters used to play similar ones, covers of top 100 pop tunes produced for the under-twelve crowd.

"Eli?"

He forced himself to look at Sloane again. "Hey. Yeah. Hi."

The dog moseyed toward him, so Eli put out his hand, palm down, and let the animal sniff his fingers. It took a micro-second for the dog to approve before he was pushing his head into Eli's hand.

Petting was imperative, of course. No man could pretend this friendly pooch's existence away. "Hello, boy," he said warmly, and the dog's body wiggled with happiness. "You're a good one. You're a very good one."

"That's Boo," Sloane said.

Eli quirked a brow at her. "Say again?"

"Paige named him. He came into our lives before she turned two and at that time 'boo' was pretty much the word for everything besides 'mama' and 'more.'"

"Got it." But that reminded Eli again of why he should steer clear of the lady and her kid. He understood all about children and pets in a way lots of men twice his age did not. Spring break was supposed to be just that—a break from his past.

Today began his time to focus on himself and pleasures of the flesh, not concerns over a dog that needed a fenced play area and a child—

No, he was not going to think anything about the child.

So he turned his gaze back to Sloane and steeled himself against the impact of that curvy body, that curly blonde hair, that ridiculously plump mouth that would look best red from kisses or wrapped around—

*No.* Not letting thoughts like that in either.

"Are you eating okay?" the woman said, cocking her head.

"What?" He sounded like a bear.

"I've got that job, you know, to keep an eye on you." A gleam of mischief sparked in her eyes.

Shit, he almost found it as appealing as her stupendous rack.

"I don't need a keeper," he ground out, because he didn't dare share any humor with her. Keeping himself detached from the woman in every manner possible was serious business.

"Okay," she said, and he had the feeling she was still laughing at him. "But let me know if you need a hand with a stroke some time."

Was she offering him a hand...stroke? His eyes

bugged out. "*What?* What are you talking about?"

That mouth of hers twitched. Oh, yes, she was definitely laughing at him. "Stroke your jaw, Eli, so I can truthfully tell Molly you've been employing your razor. What else could I possibly mean?"

She could possibly be trying to drive him nuts. Tempt him into sleepless nights for the next two weeks when she was right across the street and he was near-desperate for sexual companionship.

If Sloane Clarke wasn't everything he didn't want to get entangled with during his bachelor vacation—*and* when his real life returned—he'd be slinging back those same innuendoes and then following up on them.

But she was and so he wouldn't.

Without another look at her, the dog, or the kid, Eli turned in the direction of home. To take a cue from that Pink song that seemed to be on continuous play, it was time to get his spring break party started.

Sloane couldn't let Eli go like this. Not when he was wearing that testy expression on his face that instead of intimidating her only made him seem more human. Manageable. A guy typically worn out by a long work week.

Last night she'd babbled and flushed hot like a red pepper but she was over all that silly physical response now. She didn't have the time or an inclination for a crush, so she'd crushed *it*.

"Eli," she called to his retreating back. "Stop a minute."

One foot in the air, he hesitated, then he squared

his shoulders and made an about-face. Boo rushed him again, clearly expecting more pets.

Which he automatically provided. "You like dogs?" she asked.

He blinked at her, as if mildly insulted. "Of course I like dogs."

"I wasn't sure."

"I've had dogs my whole life." A pained expression crossed his face. "Our last one lived to thirteen. We lost Rover a few months back."

"I'm sorry to hear that. Rover?"

"Allison drew the short straw and got to name him. She was seven."

Sloane smiled. "Rover's good."

Eli's fingers continued fondling the dog's ears. "I felt blessed at the time. The twins were going to choose Hoopsie." His free hand rose, stop sign-style. "Don't ask."

"Okay, I won't ask about that. But I wondered…" She pulled on the hem of her T-shirt and told herself it wasn't a nervous gesture. "Well, you're welcome to join us for dinner. Nothing special, spaghetti and salad. Paige loves pasta."

His gaze flicked to her daughter, flicked back. "Thank you, but no. Despite Molly's dire warnings, I'm actually perfectly capable of making myself a square meal."

"It's not that. It's—"

"And I have calls to make. I've…uh, lined up some dates for the next couple of weeks and I need to make reservations, that kind of thing. You know."

She supposed he meant reservations for dinner, what one might do before a scheduled night out with another person, but Sloane had no recent experience of such a thing. "I see."

He glanced down at the dog, then back up at her. "Maybe you have some suggestions."

"About?" she asked, puzzled.

"A place where a woman might like to eat dinner or lunch. You know."

Again with the *you know*, when she absolutely did not. "I'm afraid single motherhood has left me no time for dating," she admitted.

Now he exhaled. "So you probably get me."

She cocked her head. "How's that?" From the corner of her eye, she saw Paige stop playing whirling dervish to scoop up one of her dolls who had been lying in the dirt. Her daughter held the toy by the ankle and the skirt of its dress fell toward its head. Sloane stared, frowning. Was that a pair of her own panties twisted around Baby Sally's waist and thighs?

But Eli was speaking. Returning her focus to him, she realized he and Boo had walked back toward her house and now stood at the mouth of the pathway leading to the front door. Half wine barrel planters flanked the brick walk, and she couldn't help but notice that the purple petunias she'd planted looked thirsty. In the way of mothers everywhere, she multitasked by jogging to turn on the water at the hose spigot and then jogged back, dragging the length of green tubing across the yard, water flowing weakly.

"You were saying?" she asked Eli, and noted the glazed look in his eyes.

Registering moisture, she glanced down to see that during her manipulation, the hose's nozzle had dribbled on the front of her shirt. The cotton had gone wet in two places, a dark splotch over her ribs and another over one nipple. To her mortification, the tip of her breast stiffened even as she forcefully willed it not to react.

Damn. Heat rushed her face, red pepper all over again.

"Um…" She glanced back at Eli who now seemed fascinated by the dog. "Uh…"

Her cell phone vibrated in her back pocket.

Saved!

But upon glancing at the caller she realized this was no reprieve, not in the least. With one hand she accepted the call anyway, because avoidance only served as another tick against her.

She figured Diane Dunlap kept a handwritten list of Sloane's sins.

"Hello," she said, voice cheery. "How are you and Jeffrey?"

There followed the usual polite back-and-forth. Diane had country club manners and Sloane could picture the older woman, her platinum hair just so, her manicure pristine. "You want to talk to Paige?" she repeated, loud enough for her daughter to hear. Paige immediately glanced up, then shook her head with vehemence, clutching Baby Sally to her chest. "I'm sorry, Diane, but Paige's taking a late nap. Perhaps we can call tomorrow—"

Her daughter's grandmother interrupted with her opinion on late naps and how Sloane's laissez-faire parenting style would cause them all great distress later on.

Though she knew the older woman had no claim to a perfect record herself considering her son's reckless adult life, Sloane still felt her shoulders slump as the criticism pierced her weakest spot. It barely registered when Eli slipped the hose from her hand and took over the watering. She wiped her damp palm on the leg of her jeans and made an effort to change the conversational direction, interrupting Diane midstream.

"We're looking forward to you visiting Sawyer Beach at the end of the month," she said, infusing her words with every bit of positivity she could muster. "Paige will love to show you her artwork on the walls at Cozy's."

For some reason, Diane didn't object to the hours Sloane had her daughter in Cozy's Daycare while she worked at a small accounting firm as a bookkeeper. The older woman liked visiting the center and preened at the praise the staff shared with her about Paige. One might have thought the compliments were earned by Diane herself—certainly she considered them a reflection upon her, in any case.

The call continued, Sloane deflecting complaints or criticisms whenever possible by asking about Diane's husband, Jeffrey, or telling an amusing story starring Paige. It would have helped if her daughter had been willing to get on the call, but she was often cowed in the presence of her larger-than-life grandmother and even hearing her over-loud voice through the phone could turn Paige shy. In the morning hours there was a better chance that the little girl would forget some of her self-consciousness and respond more naturally.

"What can I do to ensure you have an enjoyable stay while you're in the area?" she asked. While Diane and Jeffrey had once lived in the nearby larger city of San Luis Obispo, they'd moved to Florida along with a group of friends to a gated community and golf course living. Of course, they'd lived in a gated community on a golf course in SLO, but the lure of their friendships had been stronger than that of staying near their married-with-no-children daughter as well as their granddaughter, born of a woman whom Diane had never considered right for her son.

*Not good enough.* That was the actual phrase. Sloane had never been good enough for JJ— Jeffrey Junior.

Though truth be told, JJ had never completely pleased Diane either, despite her love for him and how she'd been blind to most of his faults.

Those faults that she had acknowledged she'd consigned to a blame bucket labeled with Sloane's name.

"We've decided to stay in Sawyer Beach to be closer to Paige," Diane said now, "instead of being with Rona at our old house."

"Oh, wonderful," Sloane managed to choke out, even as dismay overwhelmed her like cold water rising from her ankles to the top of her head, drowning her. "Though I'm sure Rona will miss her time with her mom and dad."

"Our priority is Paige," the older woman told her. "Now that she's nearly four, we intend that she comes to know us *very* well."

Sloane heard the words as a warning. From the very beginning, Diane had made veiled references to taking her daughter from her, and as the call wrapped up, Sloane couldn't ignore a bone-shaking anxiety.

She needed to hold her child. Stat.

Starting toward Paige, she blinked a couple of times, bringing the bigger picture into focus. Still occupied by Baby Sally, Paige was trying to stuff its splayed plastic fingers into the sleeves of a pink dolly coat, seemingly oblivious to the adult on her left. Eli.

Sloane's heart lurched, jolted by the sight of the man, who'd apparently finished watering and was now sitting on the same porch step as the little girl. He looked at ease, relaxed in his own skin.

And the right age to be Paige's father.

Seeing them together… Sloane took in a breath and thought it through. It looked…nice, she decided.

Definitely not threatening, like Diane's call.

As she drew closer to the pair, Paige made an irritated sound, frustrated with the task of dressing Sally. Without missing a beat, Eli reached over to pluck the toy from the little girl, his big hands deftly fitting the garment onto the small toy, even to the point of fastening tiny buttons into the tiny buttonholes.

Sloane stared, as did Paige, who slid her little bottom closer to the man.

"I want to let you know I've been nonstop parenting pretty much for the last eleven years," Eli said, his gaze still trained on Baby Sally.

"Um, yes?" Sloane had heard this from the twins.

"So I have this idea of looking for a little fun during the next couple of weeks while my sisters are gone," he continued.

"Right."

He passed the doll to Paige, who took it without hesitation and also didn't move away from her spot pressed to Eli's side as she began fussing over Baby Sally.

"I'd be grateful if you wouldn't report back to them on my…" He seemed to think. "Comings and goings."

"Oh, of course," Sloane answered immediately,

guilt pinching as she remembered what she'd promised Molly, but only as a way of gently making fun of her brother.

"Great," he said now, getting to his feet and starting up her walkway. "Thanks."

Boo and Paige trailed behind the man, then so did Sloane, feeling guiltier by the footstep. As he prepared to leave her property, she called his name.

He turned then, looking at her little tribe of dog, child, and plastic Baby Sally. Sloane took the opportunity to study him as well, a man in his prime with a face to inspire sighs and a body to launch daydreams. Her heart beat a little faster despite herself but she ignored the pitter-patter of it just like she ignored the traitorous heat kindling in her belly.

"I would never…" Sloane began, and then cleared her throat to start again because he deserved her assurances. "I'm sorry if I gave you the wrong impression. I won't say a word to them. I just couldn't resist teasing you a little bit yesterday."

"Good." Then his eyes narrowed. "But you seem to have lost your sense of humor now—after that call."

Could he tell? She bit her lip. "Well…"

"Is everything okay?"

She resisted the urge to unburden herself. He was a stranger, and a man who wanted to focus on fun, not a single mother's persistent fears.

"It's all great," she said, plastering on a smile. "You go on now and have a good night." Paige tugged on her shirt and she looked down, into her daughter's face. "Did you want to say goodbye too, Paige?"

"Baby Sally," the little girl said.

"Oh." Without thinking, Sloane played along as

she always did, and looked to Eli. "Baby Sally wants to—" Then she broke off, not sure if he'd enjoy being part of the game.

He didn't skip a beat. His gaze shifted to the doll Paige held up. "Goodbye to you, Baby Sally. I hope you enjoy your spaghetti dinner."

"And ice cream for dessert," Paige added.

"And ice cream for dessert," he dutifully echoed in a grave voice.

"Kiss," Paige said now, and pushed the doll toward Eli so he had to grasp Baby Sally, his big hand wrapped around her bare plastic thighs.

He flicked a glance at Sloane, then gave a peck to the top of Sally's wealth of unkempt brown hair. When he tried to return the toy, Paige held out her hand instead, like a princess meeting a knight. "Kiss," she demanded.

Bending, Eli pecked her knuckles. "Uh, thank you, ma'am," he said straightening.

Sloane had never seen her daughter take such a shine to a stranger, so she wasn't prepared for Paige's next command. "Kiss Mama!" she declared, imperious.

Eli's gaze met hers and Sloane felt that burning, red-pepper heat once again crawling over all her body. "Now, Paige—" she started, but before she could finish, she felt Eli's dry lips brush the heated skin of her cheek.

Okay, fine, nothing to get excited about, but as she moved to end it and he moved to end it, they both moved in the same direction and now it was his lips on hers, almost a real kiss.

Her first kiss in more than four years.

The top of her head blew, but it was over nearly

before it started and they were edging away from each other again, this time in opposite directions. In fact, Eli practically sprang back, clearly in a hurry to depart.

Paige reached up to snag the doll from him and as it left his grasp, Sloane saw that Baby Sally's panties—no, damn it, *her* panties—were left dangling in his fingers.

*Oh, God.*

He gave one distracted look at the scrap of pink lace, shoved it in his front pocket, then stalked off in the direction of home.

Sloane opened her mouth to—

But words wouldn't come out. Her brain couldn't find a way to politely request the return of her underwear. No simple, "Hand over my panties" or "Unhand the thong!" Not with that kiss still a burning imprint on her lips and the knowledge that her crush wasn't quite as conquered as she'd thought burning in her head.

# Chapter 3

Eli held his phone to his ear as he rummaged through his closet to drag out the pair of boots the sisters had given him for Christmas. He'd been forced to make a solemn promise never to wear them to work, which tended to be hard on footwear. "I'm fine, Nora. But enough about me. Are you sure your car is running okay?"

She answered in the affirmative.

"And Lynnie and Molly? They didn't stay up too late last night watching..." What was their latest obsession? "That dress show?"

Nora only laughed.

He shoved his feet into the leather. "I take that to mean you girls have yourselves handled."

"We're on spring break. Why don't you give yourself one and stop worrying about us so much?"

Yeah. He was supposed to be doing that. And

because he heard a note of concern in his oldest sister's voice, he found himself addressing it. "I've got a date tonight, believe it or not."

"Really?"

"You bet. Don't tell the others, though, because tomorrow they'll pester me with what I wore, what she wore, what I said, what she said..." The words poured from his mouth, even though his mind was occupied with another she, other conversation.

That kiss.

Damn, he must be hard up because only that brief touch of lips had given him a hard-on that made getting home from Sloane's place a formidable task. It wasn't as if he could reach down and adjust himself with her and her little pack looking on.

And the truth was, dolls always gave him a pause, their eyes just too all-seeing. But he'd manfully dealt with them for years and he'd soldiered on yesterday too, getting Baby Sally into that coat...

And then finding himself holding a pair of panties.

They couldn't be Baby Sally's, he knew that, and he took his unexpected and unnerving possession of them as his punishment for that kiss.

Because that possession had been no accident.

God, he hoped Sloane didn't realize that he'd intentionally walked away with them.

"You've gone all quiet on me," Nora said, and he grimaced, in his memory of the kiss and what happened after, he'd forgotten being in the middle of a call with his sister. "Is something the matter?" she asked.

"Running late for that date, that's all," he lied. "She's picking me up, and soon."

"Talk to you later, then," Nora said. "And have a great time."

"I intend to," he replied before ending the call. That was the truth, the whole truth, and nothing but the truth. Wendy Beacham, a willowy brunette, had a favorite restaurant about thirty minutes south, and she'd offered to drive him in her car. Why not? he'd thought, imagining himself kicking back in the passenger seat anticipating a beautiful night while resting his eyes on a beautiful woman.

Who looked nothing like the luscious and peachy-skinned single mother across the street.

Smoothing the button-down he wore over dark wash jeans, more of the nicer side of his wardrobe, he walked from the large first-floor master bedroom in the direction of the living room. It was early, but he gave a cursory glance out the front window, looking for an unfamiliar car.

And spotted a familiar foursome.

Without a second thought, he found himself shoving through the front door and jogging down the steps. If he walked quickly enough, he'd meet Sloane, Paige, Boo, and Baby Sally at the bottom of the drive. They all paused upon meeting.

Shit. Eli realized he was so out of practice he hadn't prepared a motive for his interception.

The panties came to mind.

But it wasn't as if he had them stuffed in his pocket.

No, instead they were stuffed in the top drawer of his dresser and he hadn't considered returning them.

Yet.

So now he turned his attention to the dog, leashed at Sloane's side. "Hey, Boo," he said, crouching to run both hands over the dog's head. "You been taking good care of your girls?" He glanced up at Sloane, then smiled for Paige who clutched her doll.

"How are you Baby Sally?" he asked politely, taking care not to meet her creepy plastic gaze. "Are you taking care of Miss Paige?"

"Princess Paige," the little girl corrected.

Straightening, he dipped his head. "Excuse me, Princess Paige."

She smiled, clearly delighted, and he remembered his little sisters not much older than that, looking to him to slay all the dragons not to mention the monsters hidden under the bed and lurking behind the shower curtain.

Eleven years, and he'd reached his quota of dragons and monsters and now was time for other pursuits.

With that in mind, he turned his gaze to Sloane, in her usual uniform of sneakers, tight jeans, and a sweatshirt baggy enough to hide all her upper good parts, thank God. But nothing disguised her face, those delicate features, her plump pink mouth, the eyes that at the moment were almost as unnerving as those of the doll. "Hey," he said, his voice coming out softer than he liked.

"Hey, yourself." Her gaze lifted toward the sky, away from him. "Looks like rain, don't you think?"

"Yeah." He shoved his hands into his pockets, so he wouldn't reach out and take hold of that sweet chin to turn her face back to his. "I believe it's in the forecast. A spring storm."

"You're dressed up," she said, still not looking at him.

"I've got a date tonight."

She glanced his way. "That's good," she said, and her smile looked genuine.

He could see her uneasiness slip away with each breath, as if she thought another woman coming into his life meant that kiss they'd shared had slipped his mind.

That he'd found it forgettable.

"Sloane..." he said, and reached out to touch her arm. It made her jump and she must have loosened her hold on the leash, because Boo broke free and took off, scampering in the opposite direction of Sloane's house.

She whirled, yelled the dog's name, but he continued on at an exuberant pace.

"I'll get him." Eli took off, then almost instantly realized that was an amateur move. A dog this young considered his pursuit part of the game. "Hell," he muttered, slowing to a walk. "Come here, boy."

As if it would be that easy. Boo didn't obey, and happy talk, growly talk, even undignified cajoling achieved nothing.

A long five minutes in, they were at a standoff, both of them panting, the dog just out of reach, rump in the air, tongue lolling.

Trying to calm his ragged breathing, Eli felt a tug on the straight tail of his shirt. Glancing down, he saw Paige, who was holding up Baby Sally.

"She's right," Sloane called out. "Boo loves Baby Sally."

"He's a better man than I," Eli muttered, then took hold of the toy. "Here, Boo." He lifted the doll to shoulder height, then shook it, trying to get the dog's attention. "Look what I have."

Magic.

The creature moved like lightning, and he had to shove his arm skyward to save Baby Sally from a fate worse than death. Still, Eli managed to get his free hand wrapped around the dog's collar and stepped on the trailing leash for good measure, but not before Boo jumped up, depositing a couple of dusty paw prints on Eli's especially selected, date-worthy shirt.

"Oh, no," Sloane said, coming forward to reclaim her dog. "Boo got you dirty."

"It's nothing," Eli said, brushing at the marks with the back of his fingers. "I can change."

"No. It's a great shirt." She frowned at him. "I really like that shirt."

"Sloane—"

She took him by the arm. "I can get that clean," she said, towing him toward his house. "You just leave it to me."

Damn, but he liked her hand on him. So he didn't resist, tramping toward his house as part of her domestic parade. Paige still had a hold of the tail of his shirt, Baby Sally safely tucked under her arm once again. At his front porch, Sloane tied up the dog and pulled a bandanna from a pocket, then wet it at the nearest hose spigot and wrung out the cloth.

Paige took a seat on the lowest porch step and Boo, tired from his play, threw himself onto the grass with a gusty sigh. Eli and Sloane faced each other, and her hand hesitated a few inches from his chest.

She bit that plump bottom lip.

Killing him.

"I can go inside, change shirts," he offered again.

"I like this one," Sloane said, her expression turning stubborn. "You should look perfect for your first date in over four years."

"Huh?" he asked, staring down at the silky blonde hair on the top of her head. "Four years?"

"Or however long that it's been," she said hastily.

"Not quite four years." He suspected, now, where that number came from.

"Whatever," she answered in an airy voice, then brushed lightly at the marks on his shirt with the damp rag, her free hand grasping the fabric at the hem and holding it away from his skin. "Look, it cleans right up."

She flapped the cotton. "Just be patient a moment and it will dry in no time too."

"Thanks. Good." He tried to be that way himself, good, and not breathe in her scent or imagine himself sifting his fingers through the light strands of her hair to play with the loose curls.

Then she did a bad thing. With a purse of her lips, she leaned closer and began blowing on the cleaned patches.

That mouth, her mouth, shaped for a kiss.

"Sloane," he whispered. She glanced up, then froze, their gazes joined.

"Eli."

He liked his name on her lips. But more, he liked his lips on her lips. His gaze narrowed as her pink tongue emerged to lick them. His muscles tightened and there might have been some warning bells going off in his head but he didn't heed them, because the need to taste her again was more urgent.

"Sloane…" he said again, his voice deep with intent.

She didn't look away or seem the least inclined to refuse him what he wanted. A flush warmed her cheeks.

Then the friendly toot of a horn had them jolting apart.

Eli's head snapped to the right as a silver sedan pulled into his driveway. A woman stepped out of the car, a long drink of water, slim and smiling, with a sleek fall of brunette hair. For a moment he blinked at the sight, nonplused.

Then he recalled who the stranger had to be.

His date.

Hell. How could he have forgotten?

But he knew, of course, and kept his attention off Sloane as he moved forward to introduce himself to Wendy Beacham. She didn't have to reach far to press a friendly kiss to his cheek.

Then she looped her arm in his elbow and turned them both toward Sloane who now had Boo's leash back in hand and her daughter back on her feet. She aimed her small crew toward home, sending a vague smile in the direction of Wendy and Eli.

"Who is this?" his date asked in a puzzled voice. Obviously she'd caught a glimpse of him and the other woman all up close and personal. "One of your sisters?"

Eli opened his mouth, but Sloane beat him to the answer.

"Nobody important," she said, without looking their way. "Just the mom from down the street. You two have a wonderful evening."

Sloane held the refrigerator door open as Alice Ricci, one of the owners of the accounting business where she worked, and who was also her landlord and friend, unpacked cold goods from a plastic bag.

"Almost a half-gallon of milk, and this cheese will go bad before we get back from vacation," Alice said. At the office she invariably wore dark slacks and a tailored jacket, but today she was dressed for RV travel in jeans and a rain slicker over a Duffy's T-shirt. The whole town had them from a promotion the market ran some months before. "There's lettuce and yogurt and a few of those apples that Paige likes."

That last confirmed Sloane's suspicions that Alice hadn't just brought things from her own kitchen that might spoil while she and her husband Joe were out of town for almost two weeks. She'd also made a special stop at the grocery store.

Then a small cardboard box was withdrawn from another bag. "And here are those oatmeal and raisin cookies that she likes. From the farmer's market, fresh today."

Not just a special stop at the grocery store, Sloane realized, shaking her head. "Alice, you shouldn't—"

"They're healthy," the older woman declared. "Oats. Raisins."

Plus butter and sugar, but Sloane wasn't objecting to the treats. "I meant you shouldn't always be buying things for us."

The older woman drew herself up and put her hands on her hips. "Paige has a special place in my heart and I'm not apologizing for that."

Sloane had to smile. Alice and Joe were retirement age, but they said that until their son and daughter started producing their own sons and daughters, they had no reason to step down from the business they'd run for over thirty years. It was a miracle they'd decided to take time off after surviving the latest tax season. A skeleton crew, including Sloane, would keep things running, though they'd also been encouraged to cut back their hours. The couple had decided that after weeks of overtime, everyone needed to recharge.

"Then thank you," Sloane said now. "Paige will appreciate the cookies…after lunch."

That last was for her daughter's benefit, who had looked up from the crayons and coloring books set out to keep her occupied on this wet, gloomy day. The expected storm had roared in at dawn.

"Is it safe to start out on your drive today?" With a frown, Sloane cast a look outside the windows which showed rain coming down in continuous sheets.

"You know Joe," Alice said, and crossed over to the small kitchen table to kiss Paige on the top of the head. "Always sticks to the plan."

"Well, be careful," Sloane cautioned, following her friend toward the front door, Boo trailing them.

"Will do." Alice cast a glance toward the ceiling. "And Joe asked me to tell you when we get back he's going to look at your roof again. The man who's painting the inside of our house while we're gone has a brother-in-law looking for work. We may have the entire roof replaced, if necessary. Any sign of new leaks?"

"Don't you worry about my roof. It's vacation time," Sloane said, instead of admitting that as a precaution she'd put a pot on the floor in the tiny back room, under where there'd been a leak before. Probably in an abundance of caution, she'd assured herself, because a month ago Joe had been up on the roof and replaced the worst of the shingles.

Alice leaned in to give Sloane a quick squeeze.

"Enjoy yourself while we're away and don't make yourself crazy worrying about the upcoming in-laws' visit. Relax some, okay?"

Stretching a smile across her face, Sloane agreed, and spent the rest of the day doing laundry, coloring with Paige, and watching two Disney movies back-to-back, a special treat for them both. The heavy, unrelenting rain prevented them from getting outside to work off her daughter's physical energy, so it was past bedtime before she managed to get the little girl finally settled beneath her covers.

But once Paige nodded off, Sloane took to the living room with her manicure/pedicure kit—a shoebox filled with items purchased at Target—her face clean and shiny after the application and removal of a goopy mask she'd slathered on—from a foil pouch also found at Target, on the shelves of the discount end cap. With Boo settled on the rug and the TV tuned to an investigative series, this episode focused on a mysterious poisoning case, Sloane lined up her polish choices, ranging from a tasteful mauve to a hot pink she'd only ever painted on Paige's tiny fingers and toes, per her insistent request.

For herself, Sloane couldn't remember the last time she'd done anything more than the rudimentary grooming of her nails. But now she gave the available colors a serious study. A spring shade, she decided, pushing aside one she remembered wearing the Thanksgiving when she was heavily pregnant.

Red wouldn't work, because it didn't shout spring and because she didn't have a bottle of scarlet polish. But mostly because she'd noticed Eli's date wearing that color.

Head bent as she filed and buffed, Sloane recalled

the tall brunette, how she'd been smooth and shining from head to toe. Her look had matched Eli's, two beautiful single people prepared for a carefree night out.

He deserved that, she reminded herself. He'd explained himself that after eleven years as head of the King household he wanted a couple weeks of unfettered...*comings and goings*.

His exact words.

The brunette was the exact type of woman to provide that for him.

*Comings and goings.*

An unbidden smirk took over her face, but it felt less like humor when she acknowledged the iron grip her hand on the small bottle of medium-pink polish. To throw off her budding crankiness—Alice had instructed her to relax, remember?—she got to her feet, waving her hands in the air to dry her nails.

The rain pounded on the roof as she moved down the hall to check on Paige, Boo's nails clicking on the hardwood floor as he followed. She widened the gap made by the half-open door, leaned against the jamb, and in the glow of the princess nightlight enjoyed the sight of her sleeping daughter. Her ill-humor eased and she knew she smiled.

What was more satisfying than this? Her little girl safe in dreamland, their cozy cocoon of a cottage sheltering them both on a dark and stormy night. What else did a woman need?

At this moment she could only thank JJ for being part of the creation of their precious child. He'd been impulsive and reckless and irresponsible. She'd been vulnerable and naïve and much too young to have a baby.

But in the last years she'd found new strength. A new confidence in herself. Maybe JJ would have grown too, and she liked to think he would have come to love Paige and appreciate fatherhood, no matter that he'd railed against the idea in the last days before he'd left her, six months pregnant and scared witless.

She'd made it through the birth alone and those first long nights with an infant, determined to do her very best for the life she'd brought into the world. Every sleepless minute had been worth it, she thought, fondly gazing on Paige's tousled strands of white-blonde hair.

"Thank you, JJ," she murmured. He'd been snorkeling in Belize when she'd gone into labor and she was still recovering in the hospital when she'd gotten word that he'd drowned in an accident she suspected was drug-related.

Sloane didn't hold any of that against him now. At the thought of her late husband, only sadness welled and she hoped he'd found peace somehow, somewhere. "Sleep well, old friend." He would always be that in her mind, a friend, because at the beginning one reason he'd thought to marry her was to save her from being alone in the world. She'd agreed because she'd been so eager to love and be loved in return.

Neither of them anticipated how those intentions might go wrong.

"Mama?" Paige's eyes suddenly opened and her gaze moved to Sloane. "Mama, is it morning?"

"No, baby," Sloane said, crossing the rug to perch on the edge of her daughter's bed. Boo came along too, and rested his chin on the mattress. "Close your eyes and go back to sleep."

Paige obediently snuggled deeper into her pillow, one hand groping for the stuffed bunny, Bun, that was her usual sleeping companion. Then her eyes flipped open again and her brow furrowed with worry. "Mama! Where's Baby Sally?"

The question struck Sloane's heart with a new fear, a fear that every mother had experienced or heard tell of.

The Fear of the Missing Beloved Toy.

She made a mental scramble, trying to recall when she'd last seen Baby Sally. Since she wasn't a usual bedtime plaything, they'd not rounded her up during the bath-to-pajamas transition. "Don't you worry," Sloane said. "I think she might be having a snack in the kitchen."

"A snack?" Paige said instantly. "I want a snack."

*Bad move, Mama*, Sloane scolded herself.

"Not now. It's too late." Tucking the covers more firmly around the little girl, she said, "Wow, what about that rain? It's like a lullaby, don't you think?"

Paige cocked her head as if listening hard and Sloane smiled, stroking her daughter's hair with a reassuring hand. "Now just go back to—"

The sound of shattering glass interrupted.

The house plunged into darkness.

Sloane shot to her feet, her heart in her throat. Boo *whoofed*.

"Shh," she told him, trying to focus. Nothing but the incessant pattering of the rain reached her though, and it wasn't a leap to surmise the storm had caused the loss of electricity. A neighborhood power outage, perhaps.

"Mama?" Paige asked in a small voice, sitting up.

"You stay put, baby," Sloane said, glad she'd not

gotten around to painting her toes, so her shoes were still laced on her feet. Patting the mattress, she ordered the dog onto the bed. "There's broken glass somewhere."

Hands outstretched, she blessed the smallness of the house which meant she didn't have far to go to find the flashlight she kept in the kitchen. Its sweeping beam revealed nothing amiss—except the loss of power—until she played it around the tiny room at the rear.

She recalled she'd left the overhead fixture on there after retrieving her manicure supplies from its narrow closet. The light had gone out, and the old-fashioned glass globe—old enough to be retro—had broken. Pieces lay on the ground while water steadily dripped from the remaining metal parts attached to the ceiling. Playing the light over the spot, Sloane stared up, uneasy.

The persistent trickle—just missing the pot she'd set on the ground—didn't bode well.

She needed to sweep up the glass, collect towels to mop the wet floor, and devise some way to patch the hole in the ceiling.

After ten o'clock at night, with her landlords out of town, and a meager amount of cash on hand.

Running through her options, she strode back to her daughter's room, intent on ensuring the child would stay in bed while she did some initial cleanup.

"Paige—"

"Did you find Baby Sally?"

Sloane's sinking heart took another dive.

Electricity out, leaking roof, no idea how to manage the necessary repairs.

And a missing Baby Sally.

*Oh, God.*

Sloane paused, all at once seeing the doll quite clearly in her mind's eye. The last time she'd been aware of the toy had been yesterday, seconds before she'd thought Eli King might kiss her again. Right before his date had arrived.

Crossing to Paige's window, she hooked a forefinger in the shade and pulled it aside to peer across and down the street.

To his house.

To Eli's house that looked warm, dry, and in the dark and stormy night, well-lit.

Like a beacon.

# Chapter 4

Eli contemplated his laptop screen and said into his phone, "What do you think about this? 'My magic hair glows when I sing.'"

The friend on the other end of the call, Hart Sawyer, didn't speak for several long moments. "What the hell are you talking about?"

"Sorry," Eli said, "I should have filled you in better when I said I needed help with these dating app profiles. This one suggests using movie quotes to describe yourself. I was paraphrasing there."

Another long pause. "You don't have magic hair that glows when you sing, and do you, uh, actually ever sing?"

"Do you suppose anyone's honest when writing these up?" Eli asked. "Face it, when it comes to anything online, it's as that same movie says, all a man has is a fake reputation. Also paraphrasing."

Hart let that lie for more long seconds. Then he began, almost gently, "Eli—"

"Crap, I know." Frustrated, he slapped the cover down on his computer. "Those aren't good choices. But can I help it that when I see 'movie quotes,' that the entire Disney princess canon comes to mind?"

"No, you probably can't help it," Hart said. "Which Disney princess movie is about the magic hair?"

Eli pulled his phone from his ear to stare at it, then returned it to position. "*Tangled.*" He sighed. "For a second there I thought you were an idiot for not recognizing it, but that would be me, right?" Other men his age had spent the last decade watching movies starring comic book heroes or action films centered around illegal street racing.

"You're not an idiot. You raised four younger sisters."

"Yeah." Closing his eyes, Eli rested his head on the sofa cushion behind him. "I need to get this right. I have less than two weeks before they're back."

"You could ask Cooper to help. He's a TV and movie buff and probably on every dating site there is, too. You'd have matches—or whatever they call it— in no time."

Eli grunted, now reluctant for reasons he couldn't articulate.

"Anyway, you found your Saturday night date on your own. Do you really need to—"

"Actually, Sophie fixed me up," he admitted.

"Ah." Hart cleared his throat. "By the way, is she doing okay? I called her to thank her for the dinner she dropped by my place last week but she won't pick up. Instead I get weird texts with acronyms I can't interpret."

Eli opened his eyes to stare at the ceiling. "You can go by Harry's. Buy a coffee. She's barista-ing most days."

"Nah. If she needs some space for whatever reason, I can give that to her." There was a sound Eli recognized, a refrigerator door opening, the clinking of one beer bottle against another. "But back to you."

"What about what you need?" Eli asked, thinking of his friend, home alone in the house he should be sharing with his now-wife. Instead, his fiancée had died of an aneurism just a few weeks before the wedding. "Is there anything I can do?"

He could picture Hart downing half a beer in one go. "I'm good," the man said.

*Right.* "I know what it's like to face a loss—one both unexpected and cruel."

"So then you understand I'm not up for a chat about it."

Eli winced. "Okay."

"Sorry." Hart's tone lost its jagged edges. "But we're supposed to be focused on you achieving your goal of mindless, meaningless boinking until your sisters get home."

"Ouch." Eli winced again. "Do you have to put it quite like that?"

"Just reading between the lines, bro."

Crap. He pressed his fingertips to the middle of his forehead.

"What was wrong with the Saturday night woman?"

Wendy. Sleek brunette. Clever. Funny. "Well…"

"Not drawn to the little you were offering?"

"Is that a crack about the size of my dick?" Eli

asked, more amused than offended. "Actually, signs were I could have interested her in a visit to my bedroom, but…"

"But?"

During dinner, she'd asked about the single mother who lived down the street, the "nobody important" that Sloane had called herself. And that had brought the curvy blonde to mind and her image had never left him the rest of the evening.

So he had to move on to another prospect, and find a way to make sure Sloane didn't get stuck in his head. He could see her even now, her make-him-sweat mouth pursed, blowing on his shirt, making his blood chug south and putting him in the mood to—

His doorbell rang, yanking him from the ledge, just before falling into that sweet little fantasy. "Hell," he said, looking toward the nearest window—outside still pitch-dark—and listening to the pounding rain on the roof.

"What's the problem?" Hart asked.

Eli stalked toward the foyer. "Let me call you back later. Some crazy person is at my front door."

Pulling it open, he stared at the company assembled on his front porch. "Sloane?"

It was the child of the group, in pajamas, a slicker over them and rain boots on her feet who answered first, a bedraggled doll clutched in her fist and an accusatory expression on her face. "You," she said, narrowing her eyes. "Let Baby Sally get all wet."

They were all all wet, Eli saw, and he waved them inside to drip on the rug. Then he gathered towels from the downstairs linen closet and piled them in Sloane's arms.

Boo the dog shook, spraying Eli's jeans, a sign he

should step back. But when Sloane threw a towel over the dog's back and then began to dry her daughter, he stepped in to pluck another length of towel that he draped over her head.

She let it hang there as she turned her attentions from Paige to Boo.

Who was going to look after her?

Setting his jaw, Eli pulled her away from her canine and began rubbing her wet hair with the towel, letting one end dangle over her face, obscuring her features. "What are you doing?" she asked, her voice muffled. She batted at his hands but he ignored them, trying not to absorb through his palms the shape of her head or breathe in the smell of her damp shampoo.

It was bad enough that a baby-scent wafted off Paige who had likely been in a bath before bed.

Sloane pushed at his hands again, then emerged from behind the absorbent fabric to stare up at him, her big blue eyes surrounded by lashes spiky from rain. "Are you trying to smother me with the towel?" she asked.

*Or strangle you*, he thought. Because that inconvenient pull she had on him was tugging at him again, making him want to explore it, explore *her*, no matter how wrong they were for each other.

As if to emphasize the fact, Paige yanked on his shirt. "You," she said again in that accusatory tone.

*Right. Me. The one having inappropriate thoughts about your mom.*

"Mr. King," Sloane corrected, then gave him a quick glance. "Sorry."

"Don't worry about it," he answered, and hunkered down to face the child at her level. "What's the problem?"

She shook the doll in his face and he noted its clothes and hair were indeed drenched. "All wet."

He looked up at Sloane, not sure why he was to blame. "It's not your fault," she said. "We must have left her here yesterday. We found her at the bottom of the porch steps."

"Ah." Standing, he took the toy in hand. "I'll take care of this," he said, heading to the hall bathroom.

Sloane and company followed him. "What are you doing?" she asked, sounding part anxious, part curious.

"Not my first doll-in-need," he said, hunting through the cupboard beneath the sink. With the blow-dryer in hand, he plugged it into the outlet and then turned it on, aiming the heated air at the doll. The hem of Baby Sally's dress fluttered and her long hair went wild. With those eyes she looked a little too much like Medusa, so he made an effort to avoid her unblinking gaze.

Being turned into stone was not on his evening's agenda.

"You've got to be wondering why we're here," Sloane shouted over the whine of the device.

Sometimes it paid not to ask. He'd learned that as a pseudo-parent, raising four girls who turned into four teenagers. That said, his instincts were not always spot-on as to when it was time to enquire and when it was not. Once, he'd found out an embarrassing detail about Nora's boyfriend's parents' sex life, as accidentally discovered by Nora and the boy. Another time he'd almost missed that Molly was struggling with a toxic frenemy relationship. Lynnie had clued him in and he'd scrambled to help solve the issue.

"We have a minor difficulty," Sloane said now.

He caught her gaze in the mirror over the sink, then wished he hadn't. Her face didn't say "minor difficulty." As he watched, she bit her bottom lip and he sucked in a quick breath of air, his belly caving.

His will to wait her out caved too. With his thumb, he flicked off the dryer and handed the doll to her owner. Then he turned to face Sloane, his back to the sink, trying to ignore the sense that he had his back to the wall too. "What's the problem?"

"I was hoping I could borrow a tarp," she said. Earnest eyes met his. "Then we'll be out of your way, quick as a cricket. In a jiffy. Pronto, I promise."

The thesaurus repeats put him on alert. He set down the dryer and crossed his arms over his chest. "What's the problem, *exactly*?"

"Minor," she said again. "A small problem at my place. Tiny, really. If I could borrow a tarp…"

*A tarp?* For a *tiny* problem? Unwilling to trust her assessment of things, he insisted they make the journey back to her house where he would see for himself.

With the asked-for plastic sheeting tucked under his arm, Eli and the rest trooped down the road *en masse*, but this time the mass of them huddled beneath a huge umbrella he found in his garage, the kind used on the golf course. The ongoing rain pummeled the nylon fabric and added to the wide puddles on the blacktop reflecting the yellow streetlight.

When Paige stumbled in her clumsy red rubber boots, without thinking Eli passed over the tarp to Sloane and then swung up the child in his free arm. She settled on his hip and he immediately regretted it. *Fuck.* This weight he remembered much too well.

It was a weight from his past and he was

supposed to be focused on his future. Especially on the free-and-easy dozen days he had left.

His jaw dropped as they approached Sloane's cottage.

Though mainly dark, light flickered inside. Frowning, he collapsed the umbrella and let it drop to the small porch. "You shouldn't leave candles burning—" he said as she pushed open the front door, but he stopped, realizing they were the battery-operated kind, and enough of them were set about to reveal a nest of blankets on the living room couch, including a pillow inside a case decorated with the face of Anna from *Frozen*.

Yes, he recognized the character, because his sisters' Disney love hadn't died. From what he could tell it would last to infinity and beyond. *Hmm.* Maybe he could somehow use that Buzz Lightyear—Pixar, but parent company Disney—reference if he ever got back to those dating profiles.

He sighed. For some reason, at the moment that didn't seem likely. Bending, he set Paige onto her feet. Then he turned to Sloane. "What's happened?"

"The electricity went out," she explained. "I'll get it looked at tomorrow morning, but for now I hoped I could spread a tarp on the floor in the room in the back. There's a leak."

That sent him to the rear of the house with the flashlight she handed over as well as the folded length of plastic. "Hell," he muttered. If he had to guess, the leak had compromised the electrical system. The buckets and pots she'd set about were collecting the water, but he spread out the tarp beneath them and then headed back to the living room where Sloane was settling her daughter under the blankets on the couch.

"We're camping in the living room, just because," she said brightly, smiling down at her daughter.

Boo looked at Eli, his expression worried as he hovered near the kid.

"Yeah, boy," he said, addressing the dog, then raised his voice. "No camping tonight, people. Instead it's a sleepover at my house."

Sloane frowned. "Eli—"

"Won't take no for an answer," he said, picking up the child's jacket and holding it out. "We'll figure out the next step tomorrow."

Then he'd figure out how to get the image of Sloane out of his head, the way she was looking at him now with apprehension written all over her which did nothing to curb the way the idea of having her under his roof…warmed him.

Fuck, he'd never sleep a wink if he was in bed and she was anywhere nearby.

"Are you trying to be a hero?" she asked.

If she knew how he wanted to have her between those sheets with him and what he wanted to do to her there, that's not the question she'd ask.

But maybe it was best she thought of him that way, as some sort of David Do-Good. Wrenching his gaze from Sloane, he switched his attention to the little girl. "What do you say, Paige? Ready to go to my place?"

"Who are you again?" she asked. Yesterday he'd thought she'd liked him. Today, she exuded distrust. Because she sensed he had a thing for her mama? Kids were smart that way.

"My magic hair glows when I sing," he said, thinking he might get a smile out of her if she caught the movie reference.

Paige drew back, looked down at her doll, then looked back at him. "Baby Sally says you're not Rapunzel," she told him with a curled lip.

It was best that someone had the good sense to see him for the imposter he was.

The next morning, Sloane left Paige with Boo in the playroom they'd found connected to the spare bedroom where they'd slept. It held a trunk of dress-up clothes, an open basket of blocks, and shelves that stored puzzles and books of all sorts. Paige, with Baby Sally at her side, sat in a child-size beanbag chair with a tower of picture books within reach.

On the jamb of the door to the special space were lines and dates and names, the chronicle of four children growing up. Eli's heights had been noted in a solid blue of course, and the last indicated he'd been measured on his eighteenth birthday. Though Sloane knew his parents had died that year, there was no blip in the girls' data. Their heights had been noted year after year. Clearly their brother had carried on the family tradition.

She stared at those markings for a long while, pondering how something so small could seem so significant to her.

Maybe because they symbolized those two simple words. Family. Tradition.

So foreign to her but so desired.

In the kitchen downstairs, she helped herself to the coffee already brewed, and as she sipped she gazed out a window that showed rain once again coming down. The night before, Eli had told her he'd be up and out early and that he didn't expect to disturb her—he slept in the master suite on the first floor. Still, she'd been aware of his moving about even before dawn, and waited until she was sure he was gone before letting Boo roam the big fenced backyard for his morning needs. Once the dog's business was complete, she'd returned to bed to snuggle with Paige until her daughter stirred.

Now the day lay ahead. Eli assured her he'd made a call and a friend in the construction business would be assessing the situation at her place as soon as possible. Because of that, she decided to postpone contacting the Riccis. Perhaps interrupting their vacation would prove unnecessary. A quick text to a coworker explained she wouldn't check in at the office today, but with their curtailed hours already planned, that wasn't a problem. Paige's daycare was apprised she'd be absent as well.

Meaning Sloane had an unexpected day off, with none of her usual tasks to occupy her. Eli had also made her promise not to enter the cottage until he heard back from the professional scheduled to look it over, pointing out that she'd gathered and carted to his place enough belongings for the time being. Then he'd added, with a narrow-eyed look, that her daughter and her dog counted on her to keep them all safe.

Yeah, he'd struck that low, so what could she do but agree?

And then secretly decide to use the free time to find out what made the man tick.

She didn't want to consider it snooping. It was merely a necessary precaution, right? She'd put herself, her daughter, and her dog under his roof, after all, and she had a responsibility to understand exactly who owned that roof. At this point it was irrelevant to recall she never would have knocked on his door in the first place if she didn't know and trust him enough through her acquaintance with his youngest sisters.

Yep, that point was irrelevant and her intended snooping wouldn't be...well, it just wouldn't be snooping.

The King house itself was expansive and charming, if a little worn. The furniture looked solid but cushions almost threadbare. The kitchen had space to spare, though the layout left something to be desired. Upon finding the laundry room, she spied a pile of the towels they'd used the night before, so she took it upon herself to throw them in the washing machine along with a few others in a basket.

The hum of the appliance combined with the drumming of the rain created a comforting sound and further exploration brought her to the entrance to the master bedroom. Through the open doorway she saw the covers on the king-sized mattress were thrown back. Framed photos sat atop a tall chest of drawers. Paisley curtains framed long windows, their simple style and blue, gold, and salmon design appealing, despite having clearly been there for quite some time.

She liked them. She liked the whole house with its traditional farmhouse style and comfortable ambiance. Glancing around the large room, her gaze caught on two chairs, upholstered in the same paisley design as the curtains, on either side of a small round table. A pair of battered jeans were thrown over one.

Reminding her this was Eli's room. That and the unmistakable hint of masculine soap and tangy aftershave in the air. She'd smelled it last night, too, when he'd been close enough to run the towel over her wet hair. Even with the thick material between his hands and her, his touch had a warming effect, dispelling the rain's chill and setting a minor fire kindling low in her belly.

Taking another breath of his scent, her curiosity urged her inside his room, even as her conscience balked. *You have no business in there. Your nosiness doesn't need to go beyond the threshold.*

But curiosity spoke again, encouraging her to explore inside. *Where else would he have stashed your panties?*

A persuasive excuse, she found, as one foot, then two crossed over.

In her pocket, her phone rang. She gave a guilty jump, then drew back on the hallway side of the threshold.

"Hey," the man in question said, when she accepted the call.

"Hey," she turned her back on his bedroom, hoping shame didn't color her voice.

"A buddy will get up on your roof, secure the situation there. But the electrical…that might be another matter from what I've described to my friend."

"Oh, no."

"Don't borrow trouble, but…" Eli hesitated. "I think you should plan on staying another night."

She grimaced. "I couldn't." Her mind tried conjuring affordable options that would accommodate herself, a child, and a dog.

"You will," Eli said firmly.

"I don't—"

"We'll talk about it when I get home."

At which time it would be too late to secure an alternative, but her will wavered, as she once again scrambled to think—without success—of where she might go. "Eli…"

"Sloane," he said, still implacable. "Another night."

"Then I'll have dinner prepared," she offered quickly. It was the least she could do.

He didn't hesitate. "Sure. That would be nice."

It was her watchword for the rest of the day. Doing things that Eli would find nice, such as clearing out the laundry room of dirty clothes—though she didn't dare open any drawers to put his away, instead leaving them on the long folding surface—and running a cloth over the furniture. She even ventured into the girls' bedrooms upstairs, again, just to dust, and noted that these had been updated, unlike the common living areas.

She imagined that each sister had selected paint colors and décor, putting their own stamp on their own spaces, making it the kind of home where it was great to grow up, where an individual was valued.

Yet still a family home, dedicated to the comfort and pleasure of the family living within its walls.

Later, Paige helped her in the kitchen by rearranging the lower shelves in the pantry. For an almost-four-year-old, she did a good job with the haphazard collection of canned goods. With what she found there, Sloane made chicken enchiladas which she and her daughter ate together at Paige's usual early hour, before Eli arrived back at the house.

He came in from the garage as they were putting their plates and utensils into the dishwasher.

Paige, suffering a sudden attack of shyness, hid behind Sloane as he strode in, looking male and gorgeous in jeans, a T-shirt with the King Nursery name on it, and a denim jacket. He shrugged out of the last and hung it on a convenient hook, then directed his attention to them.

"Ladies."

The moment felt as traditional as the house, the unsaid "I'm home" lingering in the air. It was a place for that, she decided, for dinners on the table as people came in from work, looking forward to a quiet evening with loved ones.

Before she could get too fixated on the idea, at Eli's agreement, she served up his dinner, the enchiladas and a crisp green salad, as he washed up. Then he took a seat at the kitchen table, glancing at her and her daughter, an eyebrow rising.

"We already ate," she explained. "Paige has an early bedtime."

"Ah." He nodded, then picked up his knife and fork. "This looks great. Thank you."

She began ushering her daughter to the second floor, then paused in the doorway, suddenly loathe to leave him. It was too easy to think of all the times she'd eaten alone, and perhaps he wasn't as accustomed to it, considering those four sisters he'd been raising. "Would you like some company?" she asked. "I have a short while before bath time."

"We should talk," he said, and so she took a moment to settle Paige upstairs with more toys, promising to be back before long.

Once again in the kitchen, she poured herself a glass of ice water then joined him at the table, taking a chair but leaving another between them, so as to be companionable but not too chummy.

"How was your day at work?" she asked, and felt herself blushing because the question sounded something like a query for a Mrs. King, not the next-door single mother seeking shelter. "I mean—"

"Unsurprisingly quiet in terms of foot traffic," he said, as if finding nothing amiss with her question. "The rain keeps people home. But we had our own storm damage which meant repairing some of the protection for the shade plants and cleaning up leaves and other litter left around."

"Do you get out from behind your desk to do that?" she asked. "Or are you in an office all day?"

"We're a small operation as nurseries go," he answered, "so I do what needs to be done when it needs to be done. I have a great staff…but I like to get out there and work with my hands too."

"Your father started the business?"

"Actually, it began as a sideline for my grandfather who farmed—mostly strawberries and tomatoes. But then Dad built it from a simple fruit stand to what we have today."

"You keep his legacy going." She admired that.

"I wouldn't do it if I didn't choose to," he said firmly. "If I didn't *want* to."

"Sorry." She made a face. "I didn't mean—"

He cut her off with a wave of his fork. "No, it's fine. It's just…"

Sloane thought about letting that lie, but her curiosity still ran strong. "Just?" she prompted.

Setting down his utensils, he looked at her over his plate. "Often people think I've done what I've done—taken over the business and raised my sisters here in this home, out of a sense of obligation."

It wouldn't have been intended as an insult, she thought, but she could see how others, looking at an eighteen-year-old taking on that amount of responsibility, might naturally have considered he'd felt cornered by the death of his parents. Without a choice about what he'd do following the loss.

"But it's nothing like that," Eli continued. "Not at all."

Now her internal warning signals started sounding. *Bong. Bong. Bong.* A confidence was coming. Some utterances he might not share with a random single mother.

But she shouldn't find out any more about the man, a wise voice cautioned. Safer that he remain as near a stranger to her as could be, bearing in mind he'd given her a place to sleep and she'd done his laundry and made him a meal. Because adult male companionship had been absent from Sloane's life for four years—and before that nearly as scarce—and too much familiarity might affect that meaningless infatuation she'd had for the man.

It might feed the crush on Eli she'd been managing to tamp down pretty well since arriving wet and bedraggled on his doorstep the night before.

Meaning now would be a good time to escape, she thought, to make excuses and head upstairs. But then he was talking again, and she wouldn't be rude.

"Doing what I do…if I say it was, *is*, a privilege, my poker buddies would ban me from the table." He smiled, undercutting that assessment of his friends' reaction. "And telling you it's an honor makes me out to be way too noble."

But, damn, she saw him as that now—noble—a principled, self-sacrificing, stand-up guy, who'd carried on when his parents could not. Staring at his handsome face, her chest tightened and her heart did strange things inside it, seeming to unlock and unfold like a puzzle box, making it harder and harder to breathe.

Her mouth moved, but nothing came out.

Eli didn't appear to notice. "I guess I don't have the right word for it," he said, shrugging. "It's...my life."

She swallowed, trying to modify her guppy-imitation by saying something halfway intelligible. "You, um, you've lived it, your life, in a great house."

He glanced around. "You like the old place?"

Licking her lips, Sloane nodded. "I do. And it's wonderful to think that someday your own family will add more memories to the ones stored here." How easily she could picture it. When Eli was ready, when he was finished with the long-postponed sowing of oats, he'd settle in this home with his smart and beautiful wife and begin building a smart and beautiful family.

"I don't know about someday and me and a family. I doubt it, but I'm not thinking that far ahead."

She smiled at him. That was all right. Sloane was thinking that far ahead for him. There would be two sons, she decided, to offset all the females in his life. Two tall, lean, strong sons who would know they had an even stronger foundation in their father.

"But as for this house..."

Half lost in her head and those boys she was imagining, it took her a moment to tune back into what he was saying. "The house?"

"For sure *it* won't be in my future," Eli said. "As soon as the twins get into college, I'm putting this place on the market and moving into something more suited to a single guy."

Sloane's smile died as swiftly as that fantasy she'd been constructing. Surprised, she wondered if she'd misheard or misunderstood. "You're what?"

"Moving out and moving on."

Nope. No misunderstanding. That deep certainty in his voice left her with zero doubt. He was serious about walking away and abandoning all this history…abandoning the love that abided here. How could he? How could he walk away from all this for something sleek and modern with…with a trash compacter, probably, and one of those keg coolers in the kitchen and…

"Hey," Eli said, concern crossing his face. "Don't look so sad." He reached out to take her hand.

She stared at his, how it cradled her smaller one, how the fit looked so natural, how the touch seemed innocuous and didn't betray that it caused a ribbon of heat to unfurl throughout her system, a sweet burn that any woman would recognized as trouble.

Because it was concrete proof. A demonstrable fact that no matter what she learned about the man, no matter how he shattered her illusions and poked holes in her daydreams, so far none of that was killing the crush she had on him.

# Chapter 5

The sound of heavy footsteps in the hallway reached Eli's office. He looked up, unsurprised when his friend Boone appeared in the doorway, wearing clothes appropriate for a construction site, including a pair of shit-kicking, steel-toed boots.

He gave them a study, then transferred his gaze to the other man's face. "What the hell size shoe do you wear again? You could stomp my Jeep to a pancake in those."

Boone ignored the question and threw himself into the chair across from Eli's desk.

He winced. "Christ, be careful. I don't want my office furniture turned into kindling."

"What's got you so cranky?" Boone demanded, frowning. "You were supposed to be riding high with the sisters on vacation. You mentioned something about striving to get your dick wet as often as possible."

He glared at his old friend even as guilt tasted sour on his tongue. Yes, that might be a crude-but-true version of a goal he perhaps had articulated on a poker night before Nora, Allison, Lynnie, and Molly had left town, but even when the cards were being dealt he kept it cleaner than most of their friends. "I don't talk shit like that."

"Okay, you don't," Boone conceded. "But word on the street is you're wasting no time in the pursuit of your heart's desire."

Eli glanced at the paper cup of something steaming in his friend's hand, the logo on its side making clear he'd stopped at Harry's, the coffee place in downtown Sawyer Beach where he'd likely encountered their favorite barista. "You mean you had a word with Sophie."

"Was that where I heard it?" Boone titled his shaggy head in a vain attempt to look uncertain. "Maybe, but—"

"Shut up, just shut up," Eli muttered, fully aware he was being needled, but unable to curb his response. Christ, he *was* cranky. On a sigh, he decided to start over.

"Hello, Boone," he said. "How's your day so far and what brings you to my office on this fine morning?"

The other man glanced out the window that showed the deep blue sky and scuttling clouds. He returned his attention to Eli, and with a shrug seemed to indicate he was willing to go along. "You asked me to take a look at the house across the street—I was there first thing this morning. By the way, the back door was open, but I locked up after I left."

"Shit," Eli said, disgusted with himself for not double-checking.

"Frankly, there wasn't much to steal." Boone rubbed his palm across his gritty jaw. "Even the TV…"

"Yeah." Eli had noted the Spartan surroundings himself. The young single mom probably kept the household going on a shoestring. "What can you tell me about the storm damage?"

"I'm sorry I couldn't get to it until today, but what you managed yesterday with your foray onto the roof—"

"I did what I could before work."

"You did well. I added another tarp and tacked it down so even the briskest wind won't dislodge it. But the electrical…" He shook his head. "It's old school, Eli, and the service panel is shot. I think there's a whole replacement and rewiring job in the future."

Shit. "So Sloane won't be moving back anytime soon."

The other man shook his head. "Not if she likes lights on."

"Damn." He tapped a pencil on the desk. She'd tried calling her landlords the night before but they were on vacation in an RV and were likely out of cell phone range as they traveled through the desert.

"She's going to have to move until the updates and repairs can be completed," Boone said, exactly what Eli was thinking.

"Damn," he muttered again.

"Maybe she has family in the area."

He didn't think so, because he thought she'd have mentioned it, but he realized she'd not talked about herself and her background much at all. Head down, he studied the dents and scratches in the battered surface of the painted metal desk. Yeah, she'd been playing it pretty close to the vest. Not even a peep about her daughter's daddy.

"I suppose you can offer her lodging at your place until her landlord returns," Boone mused.

"What?" Eli's head shot up. "That's not gonna happen."

His friend lifted both hands. "Okay, just checking. I thought maybe you'd finally got a good look at her and changed your mind."

"Huh?"

"I saw her once at your place, remember? Then, you said something about taking a hard pass." A crafty light entered Boone's gaze. "But now...maybe you *have* taken a second look, yet you're afraid—"

"I'm afraid I'm going to have to punch you in the head." Eli glared.

"You're telling me your sweet single mom isn't tempting you in the slightest?"

Eli straightened in his chair. "This is not about..." Her impressive breasts, her scent, that brief but startling kiss they'd shared.

"Not about?" Boone prompted.

"Sloane is..." Eli frowned. Damn it, the woman was not affecting him and no one was going to get the impression otherwise. They were on two separate life trajectories. "Sloane's a local in need of a little assistance, nothing more."

"Okay," Boone agreed. "And you're right, her problem is not your problem. It's not up to you to give her the keys to the—heh—Kingdom."

"You're so funny."

Boone appeared pleased. "I thought so. King—

Kingdom. I can't wait to tell Gemma tonight."

Eli tried withering him with a look. "I already gave Sloane a set of keys and the fact is, she's really not a problem for me. The house has six bedrooms, for God's sake, and I work long hours."

"Yeah, but won't it cramp your style? You've said you want—"

"I'm not planning orgies in the family room." He set his jaw. "For the time being, my sisters still call the place home, you know."

"There's the child, though," Boone said in a reasonable voice. "She's gotta be annoying. Demanding. Loud."

"No. She's a little kid." Cute, and stand-offish at times, but Eli mostly blamed Baby Sally for that.

"You've already raised little kids," the other man pointed out. "I thought you were looking forward to a break."

"And there's a dog," Eli said, suddenly desperate to shut down the conversation. "Boo makes it all worthwhile."

"Why didn't you say so in the first place?" his friend raised both hands again, then got to his feet, his lips twitching. "Since there's a dog named Boo, I'll say no more. Give me a call if you need anything else."

He strode from the office next, leaving Eli vaguely irritated and not-so-vaguely sure he'd just been played—reminding him a little too much of how he'd goaded Boone about his Gemma back in January. But instead of dealing with either feeling, he decided to focus on work, and didn't look up until another set of feet quick-stepped down the hallway a couple of hours later.

A figure appeared in the doorway.

One look, and without thinking, Eli got to his feet.

Before, he'd seen Sloane in jeans and sneakers. Now she wore something filmy and flowery and fluttery, a long-sleeved dress, that veed at her collarbones and wrapped at her waist. It ended just above her knees, but her calves were sexy enough, thank you, especially when her feet were slipped into a beige pair of high heels.

Her plump mouth was rosier than ever and she'd done something to her eyes…he couldn't look away from them once their gazes met.

"Hi," she said, sounding uncertain as she lingered outside his office. "I had a few hours to put in at the office this morning."

She'd explained she was working limited hours at a small accounting firm in town while her bosses were on vacation. Hired originally as a receptionist, she'd taken some online courses and now did basic bookkeeping tasks as well as managing the office.

"But Paige is in daycare until five." She took a few steps inside, getting close enough that he could see a tiny beauty mark at the side of her mouth. "So I thought I'd stop in to find out if you'd heard anything about my house."

With his focus on her delectable lips, his office space seemed suddenly too small, even smaller than when mountainous Boone had occupied one visitors' chair. Eli gestured with his arm. "Would you like a tour?" He glanced out the window noting the mix of sun and clouds. "I can lend you a jacket."

She let herself be directed toward the exit, and ignoring the interested looks from the front office staff, he ushered her out the double doors to the nursery grounds, his denim jacket thrown over her shoulders. He noticed her taking a surreptitious sniff of the collar, grimaced.

"I may have worn that while moving some bags of fertilizer."

Her face turned pink. "That's not it...it smells like you."

"Oh."

"And I'm not accustomed to male...smells." She slapped one hand on her forehead. "Did that come out wrong? That came out wrong."

Laughter eased the tension that had gripped the base of his skull upon her entry into his space. He sucked in a breath of fresh air, cool, clean, and with just the barest hint of salt from the ocean a couple of miles away. "Would you like to see the vegetable seedlings?"

She obediently headed in the direction he indicated. "What I meant was, your jacket smells like your aftershave. I like it."

Okay, good to know. But it also provided a convenient lead-in to a subject he'd yet to broach. And under the circumstances, he told himself it was a natural question. "When you say you're not accustomed...well, has Paige's daddy not been in the picture for a while?"

"We were...separated at the time she was born. And then he died in an accident without ever getting a chance to meet her."

"I see. And I'm sorry. What about other family members?"

"I don't have any," she admitted, pausing to touch a fingertip to a tender shoot, the beginnings of a zucchini plant. "There's my in-laws, though. Paige's father's parents who live in Florida."

Okay, so he'd been right when he told Boone he suspected she had no relatives in the area. With that information obtained, he switched topics, and explained the layout of the nursery. In the distance he could see one of his younger workers surrounded by a passel of school-age kids, maybe first or second grade. Another group of them with another staff member gathered by the flowering shrubs.

That field trip, he recalled, and walked her toward some of the most interesting hybrid citrus trees. "You can get an orange, a lemon, and a lime, all three grafted together," he said. "It's known as a cocktail tree."

Without warning, she grabbed the hand he'd used to gesture. "What aren't you telling me?" she asked, her fingers cold on his, her gaze trained on his face. "I can tell you're stalling."

Yeah, he was. He turned his wrist, so that his warm palm met her cooler one. He squeezed. "It's going to sound like bad news."

Her eyes briefly shut. "That means it *is* bad news."

Eli gentled his voice. "It's not safe to return there, Sloane. The damaged roof might not hold up. At the very least, you'd have to do without electricity."

She bit her bottom lip, her eyes opening though her gaze appeared unseeing now, as if looking into a distance where he couldn't follow. "Okay." Her voice sounded a little shaky, a little weary, but she slipped her hand from his hold. "I'll think of something—"

"I'm already working on that," Eli assured her, thought processes moving at warp speed. "You and me…together we can figure something out."

Her eyes sharpened again, pinned him. "No," she said, shaking her head. "You can't do anything more for me."

"Why not?"

Instead of answering, she was on the move, speeding in the direction of the exit in those high heels. "Because," she said over her shoulder.

"That's no answer," Eli retorted, already frustrated, and then lengthened his stride to catch up with her. Reaching out, his hand found denim. But when she yanked her arm to loosen his hold, her shoes slipped on a skim of muddy ooze left over from the storm. As she lost her footing, instinct made him lunge for her with his other hand too, and then he jerked her close, righting her balance.

Steadying her against him, her back to his chest.

They were both breathing too hard, but it wasn't from exertion. He knew that. Emotions were running high as he turned her, fingers gripping each of her shoulders. "Sloane," he began, his protector instinct taking over, a compulsion honed by eleven years of being in charge.

Only one reasonable path out of her dilemma presented itself, and he prepared now to make the case.

"Sloane," he began again, staring into her face.

But then his words died on his tongue, his brain turning off as his body registered the warmth of hers as well as the slight tremor running through it. Her blue eyes went wide, diverting his focus, and then it was her mouth, that rosy, plump mouth, that he suddenly needed to communicate with more than he needed his next breath.

He swallowed a low groan. "Sloane…" he whispered, knowing he was going to kiss her. Knowing he had to kiss her. His head bent.

His dick buzzed.

Startled by the novel response, he froze, then it buzzed again.

Revealing it wasn't his penis, but another p-word. His phone.

Coming aware of his surroundings once again—daylight, family business, children not far off—he tore his gaze from her lips and reached for the device with one hand, keeping his hold on Sloane with the other.

"We've got a problem," his head cashier said.

He nodded in grim agreement. "Yes, we do."

Sloane allowed Eli to tow her toward the structure housing his office. It wasn't fancy, but the wooden building was freshly painted a clean white and was comprised of a large area up front for customers to special order and submit payment, then a long hall that she'd noticed before had rooms on either side, desks and file cabinets in most. One had to be a break room because there was a plastic-topped table, a couch, a microwave, and refrigerator.

At the very rear was Eli's office, and that was the direction he was hauling her toward now.

She tried resisting. A moment ago they'd been poised on the brink of something dangerous, intimate, signaling it was imperative to put distance between them. "Look, we can talk later."

"Yeah, we will talk later, after I handle whatever caused Lara to call."

At the open doorway he halted, and Sloane took in the sight of a nursery employee—likely Lara—who stood over a child huddled in one of the visitors' chairs. Both woman and little girl appeared deeply unhappy. A small pile of candy bars and gum sat on the ugly metal desk.

Sloane looked from the snacks to the child, whose dirty hands were folded into a Sunday school prayer bundle. The rest of her didn't look clean either, her pilled leggings stretched out at the ankles, her thin hoodie with a front pocket stained, no warmer jacket in sight.

"What's going on?" Eli asked, his hand releasing Sloane.

Liberated, she stepped back, ducking into the hallway. Eli flicked her a quick glance over his shoulder so she didn't run like she wanted to, but whatever was happening, it wasn't her business to witness.

And the defeated expression on the child's face made her want to stick her fingers in her ears and hum.

"Lara?" Eli prompted. "What's going on?"

"She's supposed to stay with her assigned group," the woman said. "They get a tour, have a taste of some of the herbs we grow, then they come inside and we give them juice and long-stemmed strawberries."

"I know this," Eli said. "You went over it with me."

"Little missy here," Lara said, her voice turning hard, "isn't keeping up with the others."

Sloane cringed at the disparaging tone. It made her feel five again, and seven, and seventeen, judged by all those people who didn't find her clean enough, her clothes trendy enough, her living situation not up to their standards.

Lacking.

Unloved.

It didn't take being a genius or even well-fed to understand when you weren't wanted where you laid your head at night and to sense others' subtle disdain everywhere else in the world. Some strangers were just out-and-out offensive, right to your face.

"Can we reconnect her with her group?" asked Eli, then his voice changed and Sloane knew he addressed the child. "What's your name?"

"Annie."

"Lara, can we reconnect Annie with her group?"

"She said she needed the bathroom," Lara explained. "I pointed her toward the restrooms myself."

You often needed the bathroom when you lived like she guessed Annie lived, Sloane thought. It was a place of peace, away from at-home sniping or schoolyard tormenters. Sometimes you just needed to run the hot water over your very cold hands. Sometimes you needed to see your face in the mirror to remember you weren't invisible.

Once more uneasy, Sloane reconsidered that quick getaway. She could race to Eli's, pack up their things, put Boo in her car, collect Paige at daycare, and then—

It was the "and then" that stumped her.

"The child stole all these things," Lara was saying, and Sloane imagined she indicated the Paydays and Milky Ways and the packets of gum. "It's not right."

Eli sighed. "Okay, but—"

"The first time I let it go," Lara said over him. "I saw her taking one bar from the display by the register and told her to put it back unless she had a dollar to pay for it."

"I appreciate you taking your responsibility so seriously—"

"She walked out and then she snuck back in, filled the pocket of her sweatshirt and then tried walking out again, as cool as you please."

No, Sloane wanted to correct her. Annie wouldn't have been cool at all. She would have been quaking on the inside and not even sure what exactly prompted her to steal. Real hunger, a desire to have something others could so easily obtain, a need to hoard a treasure of her very own, some combination of all three.

Eli sighed. "Lara, I think we can—"

"I think we can't," the woman said. "I think we should call the police and scare this little miscreant straight."

*Call the police.*

*Scare this little miscreant.*

*Call the police.*

*Call the police call the police call the police.*

The echo became so loud that Sloane couldn't hear herself think. Her hands started to shake and then her legs began moving, slowly at first and then faster, taking her down the hall and toward the exit. Out of the building that was keeping the ugly memories much too close.

*Call the police.*

Eli may have summoned her back, but she didn't stop, she kept moving blindly, pushing past the double doors and then sucking in cool air as she kept going, nearly running now. Trying to outpace her past until she had her distress shut down, boxed up, and finally shoved back into the far corner of her head where it was supposed to stay. Likely only minutes passed, but when calm returned at last, she discovered herself far from the nursery building, half hidden in a makeshift grove of mature palm trees whose roots were boxed and ready for transplant.

With no one else in sight, she took in a few more steadying breaths, trying to recall exactly why she'd come to the nursery in the first place.

Oh, yeah. Hoping to hear she could move back to her house. Instead, she now found herself homeless, and not for the first time—but in this case she had a toddler and a dog to look after besides herself. Before that had a chance to sink in, she saw Eli winding through the rough trunks and around the spread of the palm fronds until he came to stand before her, his hands shoved in the front pockets of his jeans.

"You found me," she said, under his steady gaze now mortified by her unplanned flight. Where was a convenient hole to sink into?

He glanced over his shoulder. "One of my guys spotted you." His hand slid from his front pocket and reached behind him, into another. He produced a Butterfinger bar and held it out.

The only choice seemed to accept it. "As a way of sweetening the bad news?" she asked lightly, unwrapping the bar and then taking a bite.

He watched her chew and swallow. "Is it working?"

She ignored his question for one of her own. "Did you pay a dollar for this?"

"I bought them all, and gave them to Annie and

the rest of her group. Except this one, that is. I saved it for you."

She forced herself to take a second bite, chewed, and swallowed again. "I loved candy as a kid. I'm lucky I had teeth by time I was eighteen and saw my first dentist."

He nodded, as if absorbing the information. Then both hands swiped through his hair, tucking the long strands behind his ears. "Sorry you had to see all that. Back in my office."

"Did you call the police?" She pretended a great interest in the plastic wrapper.

"God, no. I did have a chat with her group leader and put in a call to the administrator of the after-school program—not to complain," he added quickly. "I asked them to make sure Annie's home situation is…stable."

Sloane could practically guarantee it was not, but she declined to share.

"And Lara…" Eli grimaced. "I talked with her, too, about her reaction. Those candies…she has them by the registers and the money collected goes to the Special Olympics. It's a cause very dear to her heart. But she won't do that again."

"Situation managed, then," Sloane murmured, and folded the wrapper over the uneaten section of the Butterfinger and tucked it into her purse. Chocolate didn't go well with an agitated stomach. "I should be on my way."

"Why'd you run?"

She started, not expecting the bald-faced question. Her head came up, her eyes meeting his. "I…"

"What bothered you most?"

"I was Annie, once," she heard herself confessing, and felt almost relief. "I...an older boy from our apartment complex convinced me to shoplift candy for the both of us from the corner store on occasion. Until the time I was caught."

"And he left you holding the bag?"

"I was the one with the contraband. The clerk called her boss and he insisted she phone the police."

Sloane remembered the humiliation of waiting for their arrival by the door, the clerk standing over her to prevent an escape. Patrons came and went in the few minutes it took for the cruiser to pull into the parking lot and if anyone had pitied scrawny, six-year-old Sloane, she hadn't seen it on their faces.

"They took you to the station?"

She shook her head. "No. Looking back, they were pretty decent about it. They walked me to the apartment where I lived with my grandmother and explained to her what I'd done."

Eli had gone still. "Were you punished?"

"Not in the way you're thinking." Realizing she still wore his jacket, she made to remove it, shrugging to slip the denim free in preparation for taking her leave.

But the man stepped close and caught the fabric, resettling it on her shoulders. Then he left his hands there, their warmth seeping through the fabric to her bones. "Which way was it then?"

Sloane glanced down at her feet, keenly aware of how he saw her. As a single mom, who may have had some rough patches during childhood and who was now temporarily down on her luck. But at this moment, he probably didn't consider her *beneath* him. A few words, and she could change all that. The neutral expression in his gaze would transform to…what?

Nothing cruel or cold or indifferent, that wasn't Eli King. But pity would suck too. Perhaps, even worse, she would see in his eyes embarrassment on her behalf.

But maybe that, finally, would kill the crush.

Not a terrible trade-off, she decided. With it dead and gone she could more easily move out of his house and move on with her life.

Steeling herself, she looked up. God, he was handsome. The errant thought flit through her brain as she took in his etched cheekbones and the dark, feathery lashes. Maybe she'd have to report him to his sister Molly, because there was a distinct stubble on his jaw. Yet it only served to make him look more masculine to her. More attractive.

As appealing as the warm light in his eyes.

That she was about to extinguish. She hauled in a breath.

"Sloane?"

"After the police officer left, my grandmother told me if I stole again, I would be sent to prison with my mother and father."

He didn't blink. "Your parents were in prison?"

She nodded. "I'd seen them only a handful of times and they terrified me, made me more scared than my grandmother who didn't hide the fact she considered me an inconvenience and an expense, a burden she'd be happy to toss out the door the instant I became of age. I think she only felt obligated to keep me around because Sloane was her maiden name."

His expression didn't change. "Shit," he said.

"Yeah." She nodded, her chest filling with

concrete and her throat constricting. "It's weird for kids when Mommy and Daddy are the nightmare monsters."

His fingers tightened on her shoulders. "Sloane, I—"

"That's why I had to get away from your office. When I saw Annie, it brought things back. And it reminded me of how much I...I want for Paige." At her daughter's name, her control broke. She closed her eyes, moisture leaking out the sides, aware she was missing whatever change her words and her tears—tears that she never, ever allowed herself—wrought in Eli. Before she could dash the moisture away, he drew her in, holding her close to his chest so that his heart thumped against her cheek. She twitched, a first attempt to break his hold, but his arms only tightened on her.

"What the hell am I going to do with you, Sloane?" he murmured.

"You're going to let me go," she said, speaking into his T-shirt. Forever she'd remember the scent of him, the security of his solid grasp. "You're going to let me get out of your life."

"I'm afraid that's not an option," he said, his mouth moving against her hair. "Your home is at my house for as long as you need to be there."

She squeezed her eyes tighter shut and refused to yield. "No. I don't need you feeling sorry for me."

"It's nothing to do with you, Sloane. I'm compelled because Boo needs a safe space. And Paige. Maybe I'm even insisting because of Baby Sally. I'm a little afraid of dolls, you see, so she'll play a big part in my exposure therapy. Does Paige have others, by the way? How about Barbies? You gotta know they're always silently throwing shade and I'd like to up my game and learn to ignore all that."

Though it sounded a little watery, Sloane started to laugh.

He meant her to, she realized.

"What am I going to do with *you*?" she said.

"Meet me at home tonight, and we'll hash all that out."

From within the circle of his arms, it was so easy to agree. And to realize that her silly crush's heart beat on, alive and well.

# Chapter 6

$Eli$ pushed through the side door taking him from the garage and into the kitchen. The dog rushed him and he took a moment to greet Boo with head and ear rubs before slipping out of his jacket and hanging it on the nearby hook. Delicious smells wafted from the direction of the range—stir-fry, maybe?

Glancing over, something tightened his chest. Nostalgia, he decided, triggered by the sight of a woman stirring food in a pan while a young child applied crayons to the page of a coloring book at the kitchen table. A sight unseen since his mother ruled this space.

In the years since, Eli had been the chief family cook, though his sisters pitched in as they grew older.

"Ladies," he said, as Sloane turned around and Paige looked up. "Nice to see you both."

In a moment of sudden insight, he walked to the

child, the small posy he'd brought home from the nursery in hand. They sold fresh flowers from a standing cooler in the sales office, and he'd impulsively grabbed one as he headed out for the day. "For you, Princess Paige."

A quick look at her mother's amused expression allowed him a moment of personal triumph. Hah. No idiot, him. If he'd gifted the flowers to Sloane, she'd prickle and go wary on him. Instead, he'd blocked that by offering them to her daughter who looked quite pleased with her present.

Making the single mother comfortable here, comfortable around him, was going to be the secret to making her stay.

"Mommy?" Paige said, her gaze riveted on the small bunch of posies, a small smile curving her lips.

Sloane already was coming forward with a juice glass filled with water. "Say thank you to Mr. King and then put the stems in here."

Paige did as bid, then looked to her mother. "I want to show Baby Sally."

Eli took a quick, surreptitious appraisal of the vicinity. He hadn't felt her creepy stare.

"Can you get the glass and flowers upstairs without spilling?" Sloane asked, explaining why Eli had deemed the area doll-free.

"Yes," Paige promised, sliding out of her seat. Then she headed toward the stairs, the improvised vase cradled in both hands.

"You tell Baby Sally I got those for her too," Eli called after the child. No sense in not currying favor when the situation presented itself.

Next he crossed to Sloane, who'd turned her back on him to tend to the food.

He peered over her shoulder. Yep, stir-fry. "Smells good."

"I hope you like it."

"I'm not picky," he assured her. "And I also don't expect you to prepare food for me."

She hesitated, her stirring hand stopping. "I've got to do my share or this isn't going to work for me. I'll buy the groceries—I have a list on the counter, please feel free to add to it—and because my hours are fewer than yours, I'll be making the dinners."

"Sloane—"

"I have to feed Paige, anyway."

"But Sloane—"

"Are you going to let me pay rent? Because I may have to be here until Alice and Joe get back."

"I realize that, and no, you may not pay rent."

"Then I'm in charge of groceries and dinner." She turned off the heat under the food and turned to face him. "Agreed?"

"Agreed," he said, grimacing. And then, because he couldn't help himself, he raised his hand to toy with one curl that hung over her ear. "You doing okay…after earlier?"

Somebody should be questioning *him* about that. Because that confidence she'd shared, about her childhood brush with the law, about her parents being monsters, had pierced his gut like a white-hot pike.

"I'm doing fine. Did the rest of your day go well?" She smiled at him, starting a brand-new kind of fire.

The rest of his day might as well have been spent in line at the DMV or collecting million-dollar lottery winnings for all he could recall of it at this moment. When he was so close to her smiling self, nothing else registered. The dress from earlier had been replaced with jeans and another T-shirt, and it would be lying to say he hadn't noticed the press of her round breasts against the soft-looking fabric.

But he kept his gaze trained on her face and those blue eyes were captivating enough. As for her mouth... Her tongue came out to touch her bottom lip and his muscles tensed, belly going rock-hard, dick doing the same. He breathed in, determined not to give away the lust shooting through his body.

Sloane swallowed, and his gaze followed the movement, lingering on the thin skin of her throat, finding himself fascinated by the pulse he could see thrumming there. He wanted to lick it, he wanted to suck on the place right below her ear, he wanted to shove his hands under that shirt and hold those magnificent breasts in his palms.

"Oh, no," she whispered.

He found his hands gripping the countertop on either side of her, their bodies not touching, but sexual energy sparking in the air between them all the same. "Nothing's going on," he said. But he was torturing himself with this "nothing," and it was like foreplay, ratcheting up his arousal with every breath she took, with every move he didn't make.

"This is going to keep happening, isn't it?" Sloane asked, a flush rising on her dismayed face.

"I can ignore it," he promised, though he was fighting the urge to thrust his cock into the cradle of her body, to notch himself against that place where her legs met and rock against her there, to torture her little clit through their clothes. "You turned on?" he asked, making a liar of himself.

Her lashes swept down to hide the expression in

her eyes. "Eli," she said in soft protest.

"Okay. You're right." He made to move away, but her hand instantly reached for him, her fingers sliding between the waistband of his jeans and the heated skin at his hip.

"Give me a minute," she whispered.

He gritted his teeth. "Whatever you need." His heart beat so hard he thought his ribs might crack. "I told you I can ignore this—if you can."

One side of her mouth quirked up, proving him a liar once again. Another rush of need coursed through his system and he closed his eyes, trying to ignore it and the back of her small fingers pressed into his skin as she held him in place.

She made a noise, soft and almost bewildered. As needy as he felt. Helpless.

And the protector in Eli lost it, driven to take care and take charge by the vulnerable sound. Leaning in, his mouth found hers. Her soft lips responded immediately, opening to the thrust of his tongue, giving him access to all that sweet, wet heat beyond. His heart slammed over and over, stealing his breath and his will, but he hung onto the counter, fingernails digging in, feet rooted to the floor, so that they only connected at the kiss, and at her touch on his belly, his muscles hollowing there now, instinctively begging for her to slide her hand lower.

To find his raging cock.

To provide some relief.

Comfort.

*Comfortable.*

The word slid between his ribs like an ice pick, sharp enough for him to gasp, rock back, breaking their connection.

He wanted her to be comfortable here, and this, damn it, wasn't the way.

"Fuck," he muttered, letting his head drop back. "Sloane—"

But an explanation or apology was interrupted by the clatter of little girl feet coming down the stairs. He turned away, giving mother and child his back as he struggled for control.

Their conversation didn't penetrate as he stalked to his bedroom and rushed across the rug to the bathroom and the sink, where he filled his cupped palms with cold water and splashed his face. He ran his damp fingers through his hair, then gingerly adjusted his dick in the denim, wary of any further stimulation.

It didn't respond, though, at the moment apparently only interested in what his house guest had to offer.

*Shit.*

Back in the kitchen, the stir-fry was being served over rice and set upon the table. He held a chair for Paige, then left to find her a couple of books and a cushion to use as a booster. By the time the little girl was sitting at table-height, Sloane was in place and he settled into his seat.

Only then did he look at her. "Sorry," he said, sincere. "I know I promised to ignore it."

She glanced at him, then back at her plate, and picked up her fork. "Would it be terrible if I admitted I'd be a little insulted if you could?"

The waiting food and alert-eared Paige precluded him having to answer. Then he realized that Baby Sally had joined the dinner table, sitting across from him where another plate might go, wrapped in some kind of lemon-yellow lacy garment. After that first glance, he avoided looking at her, but damn, her disdainful stare was an excellent lust-exterminator.

In the next minutes he even managed passable dinner conversation, asking Paige about her day at childcare and Sloane about her afternoon. It had begun raining again, so the discussion of the weather filled some time.

"Do you think this is really going to work?" Sloane finally asked, in a pocket of quiet.

"Sure," he said, hearty.

"I'm still uncertain about why you're insisting," she ventured. "Helping out a virtual stranger, I mean."

"Not a stranger." He sipped at the beer she'd put before him. "I run a small business, in a smallish community, despite our local vineyards, resident tech businesses, and thriving tourist industry. Nobody's a stranger."

She smiled. "We're all potential customers, you mean?"

"Something like that." Eli sat in his father's place at the table, and had for a long time. Not immediately upon his parents' death, but within the first year, because he thought his sisters would subconsciously understand it was his way of assuring them their family bond continued, unbreakable. Other things, ideals, beliefs, continued on too, passed from parents to son.

"You didn't grow up here, right?" he asked.

"San Luis Obispo."

He nodded. The biggest city around was twenty miles away. "It happened fifteen years ago."

"What?"

"The Great May Surprise Storm, or as some other

voices call it the, uh," he shot a glance at Paige, "Bleeping Flood.

"The nursery was threatened by a very heavy, very dangerous runoff. Word got out and people from the surrounding area showed up, bodies and heavy equipment moving plants and trees, overnight managing to save most of our inventory. I was fourteen and working my ass off, every second counting, but my dad made time to pull me aside in order to point out the power of community and to remember that the Kings owed a big debt to ours."

Her wide eyes took him in, her fork paused between her plate and her mouth.

"So call this paying it forward," he continued, "or backward or sideways, it doesn't matter. It's the right thing to do. It's what this family does. If it makes you feel any better, we help other individuals and businesses in need when we can."

Silence fell over the table then, which he thought indicated progress. It wasn't broken until Paige asked if she could take Baby Sally upstairs. "Go ahead," Sloane told her daughter. "We'll run your bath in a little while."

Eli rose, but before he could help her from her chair, the little girl jumped down from the improvised booster seat. "Bye," she said, smiling at him, displaying a full set of baby teeth.

He smiled back, pleased by this new friendliness, and it was still on his face when she snatched up the doll.

Its yellow lacy covering slipped off the toy and was left on the table, but Paige didn't seem to notice as she scampered for the stairs.

Eli, however, couldn't look away from it.

Without Baby Sally, it became clear that the yellow lace wasn't a doll garment after all, but instead a sexy stretch of fabric made to cover…breasts.

There was a moment of charged silence, then Sloane snatched it up and brought it to her lap.

Eli looked to her for a cue…could they laugh about it?

But no, Sloane's face had turned pink and her focus had returned to her fork and her plate. With care, she scooped up another bite of food.

Great, back to her discomfort.

"We should talk about the kinds of things you like to eat," she said, obviously latching on to a neutral subject.

"I'm not picky," he repeated, with a dark thought for Baby Sally whom he now blamed for his house guest's renewed unease. "Whatever you like to cook."

"I was thinking about tomorrow's dinner…" she began.

And there it was, an opportunity to make a statement. A chance to show that their mutual attraction wasn't a hindrance to him…nor was her presence in his home.

"I won't be here for dinner tomorrow night," he said.

Her head came up. "Oh?"

"I have a date."

"*Oh.*" She settled back in her chair, her pose now relaxed. Comfortable. Her expression communicated pleasure in the thought of him going out with some other woman.

Too bad it gave him none.

Sloane tramped halfway up the staircase. "Paige!" she called. "Dinner's almost ready."

Unsurprised by the ensuing silence, she continued up the steps. The playroom held a lure that completely captivated her daughter. The toys, dress-up clothes, and books were new to her and combined with the ones brought from the house across the street, they caused Paige to deeply immerse in imaginative play.

The floral pattern of the hallway runner under her feet muffled her footsteps, so she called out again so as not to startle the child. "Paige, it's your favorite. Macaroni and cheese."

"That's my favorite too," a man said, his voice filtering from two doors down. It was one of his sister's rooms, Sloane noted. Paige had the one across the hall from it, with the attached playroom. Only three of the five upstairs bedrooms were claimed—the twins shared one—so the night before Sloane had taken the very small fifth bedroom, leaving Paige and her restless thrashing during sleep to the double mattress found in room four.

Last night, Sloane had slept fine on the narrow single, not more than four or five times replaying Eli's "Bleeping Flood" story, which served as his reason to take in her and her daughter. Only six or seven times had there been a replay of that charged interlude when she'd been caged by his arms and wanted nothing more than to find herself against his strong body, breasts to chest, with their mouths fused and tongues tangling.

The embarrassing, bralette-landing-on-the-table moment she'd banished completely from her mind.

Now she turned into her daughter's room and paced the few feet to stand at the threshold to the play space. Half the dress-up clothes were tumbled out of their trunk and onto the floor, while Paige faced away from her, on her knees, booty in the air, as she rooted around for something under the bookshelf. "Time to eat, sweet pea. Mackie cheez," she said, using the little girl's old baby talk name for the dish.

"I'm serious." Eli came up behind Sloane, his presence causing her silly pulse to beat a little faster. "Macaroni and cheese is the one food I'd want with me on a deserted tropical island."

She forced herself to stay in place and not immediately turn, allowing some time to become adjusted to that now-familiar, but still-beguiling subtle scent of him—spicy soap and a hint of lime aftershave. "Not such a wise selection," she said, "considering a deserted island's lack of refrigeration and those high daytime temperatures."

"Such a level head," he murmured. "Do you always ruin daydreams with practical matters?"

"It's a gift," she said, meaning it. Under her circumstances she rarely had the luxury to ruminate about an intriguing and personal "what if" when ignoring what was meant she and her daughter might go without food and shelter. Indulging in imagination was fine for Paige, but was not something available to her mother unless it was part of her little girl's fun.

"It's sad," Eli said.

She spun to face him, to tell him he had no idea how dangerous *dreaming* might be, but the words stuck on her tongue. Staring, she brought her hand to her mouth, trying to hold back either a giggle or a gasp.

"What?" Eli said, then, "Oh." His hand found the sapphire-colored feathery boa wound around his neck, paired strangely with a plaid, newspaper boy-style cap covering his head. "I was playing with Paige."

Sloane blinked, then repeated his words, sounding stupid to even her own ears. "You were playing with Paige?"

"I came upstairs looking for the shoe shine sponge that Nora borrows for her boots and Paige asked me to join her."

Sloane barely heard the explanation, still processing the earlier statement. No one played with Paige except Sloane. Her boss and landlady, Alice, had bought the little girl her favorite foods and the occasional toy, but she'd never ventured into the world of make-believe with the little girl. Diana and Jeffrey, Paige's grandparents, only watched her at play from afar, from a chair or sofa or park bench, Diana with the air of a child psychologist assessing her granddaughter for potential aberrant behavior.

"He's the man," Paige said now, and Sloane glanced over to see her daughter had a purse slung across her chest and a chunky bracelet of plastic "gems" wrapped around her wrist. A turban perched on her head, crookedly. "I'm the mommy." Then she pointed at Boo, who lay curled nearby, his eyes closed. "And I have to brush the dog because we're all going to a party."

Sloane checked her watch. "Well, the brushing will have to wait because it's time for the mommy's dinner. And the man has a different party to attend."

Eli grimaced and pulled his phone from his pocket. "I almost forgot."

Sloane hadn't. Yesterday she'd been delighted at the mention of his upcoming social engagement. His date. Because that's what he wanted and what she wanted wasn't, as a temporary guest, to hinder him in his goals.

Not to mention harbor any further ideas about the two of them kissing again.

A sudden thought made her pause. Did that date with this unknown woman come with sex as dessert?

She ignored the question as well as a sudden burning sensation in her chest. How he ended his evening was none of her business. "You don't want to be late, Eli."

They tromped down the stairs as a group, Eli unwinding the boa as they descended. In the kitchen, he dropped it over Paige's head and almost made it out the door with the cap covering his hair before Sloane stopped him with a word. He swiped it off then held it between his hands seeming to study the pattern. "Sloane…"

"You don't want to keep the lady waiting," she said, again reminding him of the lateness of the hour. With every passing moment she felt a deeper need to get him away from her. Out of the house where he wouldn't threaten her status quo, the one in which she didn't let her imagination have any sort of sway.

But as the evening progressed, she couldn't ignore the reality that her world had changed—at least for a short while. This new place of theirs came with a man, and she'd never thought of sharing her life with a one…not since JJ ran off, telling her sorry, but he wasn't cut out for fatherhood after all.

Since then, it had been Sloane and Paige, a team of two, with their mascot, Boo. It had been enough…and busy as she was keeping things running smoothly, she'd never considered finding someone willing to take on a woman with a child. Finding someone to give Sloane more.

Following a bath, they snuggled into Paige's bed for story time. She wanted her mom to read her the "princess book" found on the nearby bookshelves and pressed it into her mother's hands.

Sloane hesitated, unwilling to fill her daughter's active mind with the idea that being royal was a state to covet or that she could depend upon someone else for rescue. Though her daughter had dolls and enjoyed playing with them, Paige also had building toys and art supplies and a fleet of heavy-duty die-cast trucks and muscle cars. To Sloane's mind, it was important the little girl learn she could do anything and be anything.

"Now, Mommy," Paige said, turning to the first page. "Read me this book."

By the end, Sloane found herself pleased. In the pages of *The Paper Bag Princess*, the main character Elizabeth showed she was no damsel in distress and was instead the hero of her own story. "I love it," she told Paige, and turning to the flyleaf, saw that Eli had given it to his twin sisters on their fifth birthday.

It would have been the first without their parents.

"The princess doesn't have a daddy," Paige observed as Sloane closed the book and set it on the bedside table. "Like I don't have a daddy."

They'd gone over this before, and she'd been prepared for questions since learning of JJ's death.

"That's right, Paige," Sloane said matter-of-factly. "You only have a mommy. But as you know, some children only have a daddy. Others have both. One of your friends at Cozy's has two mommies and one has two daddies. What's important is that children have people who love them and who will kiss them good night." Her lips pressed warmly to her daughter's forehead, and she tried to imprint everything she felt for her in that brief caress.

"I want Baby Sally," Paige said, scooting down in her covers and grabbing Bun the stuffed bunny, her usual sole favorite.

Sloane discovered the doll, now thankfully dressed in actual doll clothes, and inserted her beneath the sheets. Her daughter drew the toy closer. "E says he's scared of Baby Sally."

"E?"

"That's what I call him," Paige said on a huge yawn.

Now was not the time to wrangle over it, Sloane decided. She addressed the other issue instead. "Well, it's true that some people don't like babies."

"I don't know." Paige sounded drowsy. "He says I must have been a cute baby because I'm so cute now…"

"You were a cute baby," Sloane said with a sudden pang. Wasn't she *still* a baby?

"…but he said kind better than cute. Smart and kind best."

How long had the pair been conversing? Sloane wondered. "Smart and kind *is* best." She pressed another kiss on her daughter, this one to her soft cheek. A third was necessary before she said a final, "Good night."

"Maybe E…" Paige murmured something Sloane couldn't hear.

"What?"

"Kiss me," her daughter said, her lashes sweeping down to lie still against her fair skin. "Maybe he'll kiss me g' night when he gets home."

*Maybe he'll kiss me g' night when he gets home* played over and over in Sloane's head as she tidied the downstairs and then arranged pillows so she could stretch out on the couch in the family room. Fooling with the TV remote, she found a show someone in the King household had previously recorded. A couple looking for an urban oasis for themselves and four dogs.

The program's dialogue became a soothing drone as sleepiness descended. Sloane breathed deep, tried to rouse herself, but it was too much effort. Her body floated away, her mind leading her into a dream in which she shared a bed with a hard male body. His voice murmured, the low tones striking a chord deep inside her, causing her body to hum and her skin to heat. Her arms circled his neck and her mouth found the skin of his throat, nuzzling to get closer to his scent. She licked him there, because her dream lover didn't mind.

He proved it by groaning, his hold on her tightening. Her back landed on a mattress, her head on a pillow, and feeling a space opening up between them, she pulled Dream Lover close again, reluctant to lose this taste of another reality.

Maybe she hadn't fantasized in four years, but it was so easy to slide into this spell.

A mouth was at her ear, teeth nipping so that she arched, wanting more of the pleasurable sting. His weight half-lay on her, a delicious pressure, and she turned her head to catch his lips.

A dream kiss.

No. She chafed at the perfunctory nature of it and felt him begin to move away again. Her arms tightened, one leg wrapped around his hip, and she turned on her side to thrust her tongue into his mouth.

Dream Lover tore his lips away to end the kiss. "God," he said, and his hand slid down her back to slide beneath her jeans and panties. His palm cupped one cheek of her behind, and her skin prickled with sudden heat, a strange sensation.

A new sensation. Sweet. Urgent.

"Sloane," he said against her ear, his mouth trailing dampness over her cheek. "You don't want this."

She sank deeper into the pillow, holding his head close. A coworker had told her about volunteering to be hypnotized at a Vegas show. *I was outside my body, looking down. I was fully aware of what I was doing, but I'd lost any sense of self-consciousness.*

Her work friend had been told to read aloud a letter she wrote to Santa.

Sloane was writhing against Dream Lover. From above, she could see herself as she rolled her hips, rubbing the juncture of her thighs against the hard length of his upper leg. Her clit tingled, the pressure enough, with her denim and his denim, to stoke her arousal. His fingers dug into the flesh of her ass, taking charge of the rhythm, and he groaned into her mouth as he laid his own searing kiss there.

They were dry humping like teenagers, like desperate people caught in the same dream, an excuse Sloane was embracing. Just for now. Just for long enough to get to that high place he was urging her toward, her sex-starved body finally acknowledging a hunger it had been denying itself, always so wary about unleashing needs that would make her want things she couldn't have—excitement, arousal, pleasure at the hands of a man.

She was having all three now, and she wasn't going to put a stop to it. Squeezing her eyes shut tight, she ran her hand under his shirt, her palm exploring the hot flesh of his taut belly. His deep groan nearly yanked her from the trance into which she had willfully immersed herself and she gave him an aggressive kiss, distracting him from taking her out of the dream with words and truths she didn't want to hear.

When all she wanted was to come.

As if he knew, his hold softened on her bottom and he caressed her there instead, a counterpoint touch to the urgency of her own frantic movements, the ones that rubbed her clit against his muscle. Tearing her mouth from his, she panted, sucking in shallow breaths as her need climbed. Sweat broke out along her hairline and she clutched at his arm with her free hand, trying to communicate how desperate was her desire for release.

His mouth went to her temple. "Easy, baby," the dream lover said. "We'll get you there. Take your time."

Single mothers didn't have time. They had obligations and responsibilities and a weariness that could sink into the bones. So she kept moving, short strokes as the climax continued building.

Almost there, she thought, relief hovering near.

Without losing hold of her behind, he slid his free hand under her shirt, then under her bra. His big palm covered her breast, gave it a light knead, then his fingers came together and he took hold of her nipple, squeezing with a delicate pressure that made her gasp. Her body went rigid, pleasure crashing through her system, and she opened her eyes just as he groaned, his body twitching once, twice. He grabbed her hand and pressed it to the bulge in his jeans, his own holding it close.

Beneath the denim she could feel him, stiff and hot, and he pushed against her hold, his hips rolling, rolling, and then he groaned again. Dream Lover climaxing too, the signs seemed unmistakable.

And the identity of the dream man was unmistakable as well, she realized, as she blinked against the half-light streaming from the hall. They were twined on her narrow bed, the fantasy she'd tried to deny herself come to life.

It was Eli King, and by allowing herself to imagine the unattainable, to experience what she'd been more than reluctant to imagine, she could only worry that surrendering to a long-blocked need might mean it wouldn't return behind the walls she'd built for it.

# Chapter 7

The sky was still dark when Eli trudged toward the kitchen and coffee in his stocking feet, desperate to fuel up with the dark brew before facing Sloane and spouting some sincere apology to go along with his half-assed explanation.

Because yeah, he was sorry for what happened between them the night before. And no, he didn't have any convincing rationale to reason it away.

His footsteps stuttered in the doorway when he scented newly ground beans and then saw the woman sitting at the kitchen table, her head bent and her body wrapped in a fuzzy robe, the material thick enough to safely pack fine china for an overseas voyage.

The enveloping fabric didn't do anything to smother his memory of her curves in his hands though. Recalling the sleek skin of her breast and ass cradled in his palms made them itch, and he curled his fingers into fists then cleared his throat.

Her head came up, her gaze steady.

"Good morning," she said, steady with that, too.

He stared, taken aback by her calm reaction. It wasn't as if he'd expected for her to go all outraged virgin on him—she'd come before he had—but they hadn't gone into the interlude the night before with any discussion first. He'd had a talk with his sisters as they reached dating age. Not *the* talk, he'd relied on the school's curriculum and his mom's best friend for that, but he'd warned first Nora, then Allison, and finally Lynnie and Molly against being swept away— that is, letting their hormones be boss and entangling them with the wrong person at the wrong time.

"About last night," Sloane began, further confounding him. "I'm sorry."

He needed coffee. Crossing to the pot, he ran a hand through his hair. "I shouldn't have carried you to bed."

She waved a hand. "That was a kindness. I'm the one who dragged you down to the mattress."

Though she kind of did, he hadn't put up much of a fight. Any fight, not really. He filled a mug, then breathed in its steam as he brought it to his mouth. He needed to wake up all his senses if he was going to be any good at this discussion of their teenage-caliber carnal encounter.

"How was your date?"

His head swiveled toward her. "We've moved onto my date just like that?"

"Sure," she said. "Unless you want to go over what happened between us move-by-move."

She'd kissed his neck on the way up the stairs, her arms around his neck, her eyes closed. He'd clenched his teeth, catching on she was in the middle of a dream, and his intention had been to put her on the bed and then bolt before she came awake.

But she'd rendered that impossible, her arms like chains, her kisses impossible to ignore, the sensation of her using him to get off…well, he hadn't had sex with anything but his hand in almost a year and those little noises she'd made while orgasming had resulted in him coming in his jeans like a fourteen-year-old. "Christ," he muttered now, feeling his morning wood stirring again.

He shook off the distraction. "I should have put a stop to it."

"Because you're the responsible one?"

A trick question, he could tell. But only one answer presented itself. "Well, yes."

"You weren't the only person there. If I wanted to save myself from you, I would have saved myself from you." She hesitated. "I worry about the other way around. That I didn't, um, give you the opportunity to exercise your right to choose."

That was so many damn words this early in the morning, especially following eight nearly sleepless hours. Last night, he'd left her slumbering and gone downstairs to toss and turn. "Sloane…"

"Mommy." Paige wandered into the kitchen in pajamas and with one hand gripping Baby Sally's ankle.

Eli cast the toy a quick look and breathed a sigh of relief that she was in dolly-sized sleepwear and a sleeping cap. Then he looked again. "Is that one of my socks on her head?"

"Want cereal," Paige said, crawling into her mother's lap.

Without thinking, Eli walked to the cupboard and pulled out a bowl. In his lifetime he must have poured hundreds of portions of cereal for small girls who looked as sleepy-eyed as this one. Smiling a little, he made for the refrigerator, recognizing another burst of warm nostalgia. Then Sloane bumped him aside.

"I've got this," she said. "We're not your chore…last night or now."

Ho! He looked more closely at Sloane, seeing the pink cast to her skin. So that was the way it was. She thought he'd stayed in her bed and been a party to her finding her pleasure as a…as a what? A courtesy? A favor for a house guest? For a second he thought about correcting her, letting her know he'd been nearly powerless to move away when she was moaning and wiggling in his arms, but hell. Why give her the upper hand?

"You could have said no," she continued in a testy tone. "You could have walked away. But not you. No, not Eli King who is always paying it forward and doing nice things for others."

"Sloane—"

"It's a terrible habit, you know, all these…these kindnesses."

He stood there, unsure how to handle this. Her quick movements betrayed a temper she'd been trying to hide.

"Everybody knows," she continued as she stomped the bowl of cereal back to the table and her waiting daughter, "that nice guys—"

"Finish last?" he asked, smirking, because he couldn't help himself.

His double-entendre didn't make her laugh. Instead, she shot him a look designed to inflict pain.

Then she turned her back on him to engage her daughter, clearly closing the discussion.

Fine. They'd both forget about what had happened in her bed.

However, their conversation continued to replay in his head all morning at the nursery. The nice guy remark, in particular, began to rankle around midday, when he contacted his sisters for an update on their trip.

Lynnie's phone was the one he called this time. She picked up and exclaimed in alarm, as if talking to someone else, "Darcy, unhand my sister!"

"What's happening," he growled, not falling for it, but unable to let it pass either.

"We're touring a sculpture collection of half-naked people and Darcy has taken the opportunity to get fresh with Allison."

Eli sighed. "I've seen *Pride and Prejudice* a thousand times with you girls, and Darcy doesn't get fresh in the sculpture room."

"You're no fun," Lynnie said. "The truth is, we're visiting a glassworks."

"Is everyone getting along? You haven't locked Molly out of the hotel room recently, have you?"

"The last time I did that we were eleven," Lynnie said, "and that was because she broke the carved squirrel you bought me at the Grand Canyon gift shop."

"Put Nora on," he commanded, deciding to speak to the oldest sister. Lynnie grumbled, but after a pause he heard Nora's voice.

"Eli?" She didn't wait for an answer. "The car has this strange knocking sound, the tiny gauge thingie on the dashboard reads 'E' and what exactly does that mean again? Also, do you suppose that Peanut and Peanut Shell truly need to be fed daily?"

Peanut and Peanut Shell were the twins, some family joke the source of which was lost to the annals of time and with their parents who'd called the girls that interchangeably since birth. It made Eli smile a little, because the use of the nicknames and Nora's other bullshit told him all was well, easing some of the concern he'd been carrying since the instant they'd walked out the door. "It sounds like you're all having fun. I hope Darcy has a friend or three, though I'm counting on you to rebuff any Wickhams."

She laughed. "I hope you're avoiding all arrogant blondes like Caroline Bingley."

His blonde wasn't arrogant, but inordinately pissed at him. He gripped the bridge of his nose, hardly believing he was about to ask this.

"Look, Nora," he said. "I have a question. Be honest—"

"Uh-oh. You remember how this goes, right? One never says yes if one's asked about the size of butts— meaning the best answer is always no, that dress does not make yours look fat."

He sighed. "I'm not going to ask you about my butt."

"Well, you have a good butt, as guy-butts go."

*"Nora."*

The burble of laughter left her voice. "Okay, you're serious. What?"

"Am I too nice?"

The hesitation on the line told him everything.

He shook his head in disgust. "Great. Just great."

"Not for a big brother, no, you're not too nice," his oldest younger sister hastened to say. "But you're so pretty—"

"*What?*"

"—that you could afford to up your asshole a little."

His jaw dropped. "I can't believe my sister is telling me this. Didn't I teach you—"

"Hey, you asked."

Maybe she was kidding him again, because once more he could hear the humor in her voice.

"It's Thursday, right?" she said now. "Poker night. Bring it up with the guys. Tell them about your worries."

He yanked on his hair. "What makes you think we discuss feelings, for God's sake? We don't discuss feelings, we discuss sports, cars, and whether certain female celebrities are better for marrying or for...for making love to."

"God." The eye roll sounded loud and clear. "There's the proof of your other problem. You can't even cuss in front of me."

"What other problem?"

"Your...well, let's call it hyper-responsibility."

His eyes narrowed. "Why does that sound like a synonym for old?"

"You said it, not me. But you're not yet thirty, and because you've been taking care of younger sisters for so long you can't even slip on occasion and say the word fuck," Nora said. "That's much too nice and hyper-responsible and..."

"Old," he finished for her, resigned. "Still, Nora—"

"And to prove I'm not nice at all...fuck," she said, and hung up on him.

For the rest of the afternoon he stewed over that

conversation too, until he left his office for Cooper Daggett's house, the designated host for this week's game. He'd told Sloane not to expect him for dinner because they ate before play, and this time Sophie, Cooper's sister, was on hand providing the food.

She sunny-smiled him as she set out platters of ribs. Beans and coleslaw lined up beside the meat on the long island of Cooper's condo. "There's my favorite bachelor," she said.

His eyes narrowed in suspicion. "How do you describe me when you set up these dates?" he demanded.

"Uh…" Sophie blinked, obviously stalling. "How do you want me to describe you?"

"Never mind." He grabbed a beer and stalked to the other side of the room, where he let himself out a sliding door to the balcony overlooking the pool.

"And my lucky streak continues," Cooper crowed, gesturing toward the lounge chairs and the turquoise water. "A new neighbor who looks great in a little red bikini."

In the distance, a woman stood and wrapped a long beach towel around herself, grabbed a book, then headed away. "She's gone," Eli said.

"She'll be back, though." Cooper looked over. "Want to make a bet on how long it takes her to go out with me?"

The bastard *was* lucky. "No."

Sophie stuck her head out then. "The other guys are here, the food is served, and I'm on my way."

Eli and Cooper went in and joined the line to fill their plates. He saw Sophie pause beside Hart Sawyer. It was the other man's first time to make it to their poker gathering since his fiancée had died. Hart bent his head as Sophie spoke to him, and she placed a gentle hand on his back. The touch didn't linger, and then she was on the move again, out the door.

The savage beast newly roused inside their old friend Hart didn't look the least bit tamed by the brief encounter. Eli had known the other man—all the poker crew—since they took Auto Shop together sophomore year in high school. Fifteen-year-old Hart had been the golden boy then, and almost that number of years later, he'd continued to be the town Midas. Successful in all ways. Known for his even temper and genial manner.

Until he'd lost his fiancée.

Things changed, Eli acknowledged. Hart's mood had been mercurial since.

With his plate filled, Eli took a seat beside Boone. The poker table had been covered with a heavy-duty plastic cloth, since the felt required protection from the ribs and fixings. The seven men downed beers and ate their meal, then the plates were dumped, the plastic rolled up, and the card games commenced.

By their designated halftime, one single poker chip sat in front of Eli's spot. Usually, over the course of play, the pots split fairly evenly amongst the group as their skills were well-matched. But tonight, between inattention and a streak of lousy hands, everyone but Eli was up. It meant digging into his wallet again or going home early.

Where he'd be tortured by his house guest who'd painted him with what she deemed a terrible habit-of-kindness brush.

"Fuck." He said it aloud here because his sisters were hundreds of miles away.

Six heads turned to look at him. They'd all left

the table and were replenishing beverages or helping themselves to the non-greasy snacks that were opened once the cards were out.

"Uh...what?" Boone asked.

"Just fuck." Eli glanced around at his buddies. "I'm a week into spring break and that's my current mood."

Cooper laughed, his amused expression quirking his dark, devil's eyebrows. "Is it time to share then? Because my new manicure girl is moving to Arkansas and I cried myself to sleep last night. Does anyone have a rec?"

Everybody laughed except Hart. "What's up?" he asked quietly.

Boone turned serious too. "What's going on with your spring break?" He didn't mention Sloane, which just went to show the kind of good friend the man could be.

"He needs to get laid," Maddox said.

"I need something," Eli muttered.

"I heard Sophie was setting him up." Maddox looked to Cooper.

Mr. Lucky held up his hands. "I don't know anything about it. Including why you'd turn to my sister to find dates, Eli. You're not as ugly as some of the guys here."

Rafael threw a pretzel at him, which Cooper batted away. "Seriously," he said. "Hit a bar, find an appealing lady, improve your mood."

"Women have needs too," Raf told him, "though I know you don't like to think that, what with four sisters. But if you play your cards right—better than you did at the table over there—you'll find one who wants the same thing you want tonight."

"I want naked body to naked body sex," Eli admitted. The clothes-on version he'd had with Sloane had only served to prime his raging libido.

"Nothing's wrong with that, buddy, it's nature," Cooper said. "Go forth and find yourself a hookup."

"With the sisters gone," Maddox added, "it's not like you have a curfew."

Eli thought a minute, then slipped his keys from his pocket. "You're right, damn it. All of you are right." With the sisters far from home, he didn't have four girls for whom to set a good example. He could seek sex without even asking someone to dinner or lunch or coffee first.

He could stay out till dawn. Later.

No more Mr. Nice Guy. No more acting like *old* Mr. Nice Guy. It was time to go after what he wanted.

Sloane heard Eli come in from the garage. Glancing at the clock, she noted it wasn't yet ten p.m. When he'd told her that morning about his weekly poker night, he'd mentioned something about arriving home past eleven.

She hadn't pointed out it was kind of him to let her know, since she'd already been feeling bad about lashing out over what had happened in her bedroom.

Nice guys…finish last.

He'd completed that sentence for her.

Did it mean he'd found some satisfaction too? She'd thought so, but found it too embarrassing to ask outright. And anyway, the crux of the matter was all the same. She'd made a mistake and made him part of that mistake—though he refused to let her take all the blame.

He walked into the family room now, his gaze finding her on the couch, under the light of the standing lamp. Papers surrounded her and her laptop stood open.

His hand forked through his hair, and the long strands lifted then fell back into place. Her fingers tightened on her pencil and she foolishly wished she'd taken more time, the night before, to play with the silky stuff. She'd squandered her single chance at it, she thought.

"What's that mad face about?" he asked.

She glanced down, seeking a convincing lie. "Oh, just a little trouble with my homework. I'm taking an online course in the latest state tax laws."

To her surprise, he dropped onto the other end of the couch, his own face none too happy. Even slouched his body was unfairly beautiful, she decided, his long legs slight spread, the ripples of his ab muscles delineated by the dark, skintight Henley he wore with a pair of new-looking jeans.

In the air, she detected just the slightest hint of his citrus aftershave.

Then he glanced over, caught her staring.

Their gazes locked and she felt heat rising under her clothes, a response unsurprising but unwanted. She licked her dry lips and his gaze shifted to her mouth, so that she remembered their kisses, the deep, intimate wetness of them—the stroke of his tongue and the scratch of his whiskers as his lips moved over hers.

He lifted his hand to push back his hair again, and her gaze shifted to those long fingers, remembering the way his hand had slid beneath her shirt to find her breast. It seemed to swell now, the tip bunching to a tight point. Unable to help herself, she wiggled against the cushions, pressing her thighs together.

She felt swollen there too, arousal bringing heat and a softening to private flesh. Tonight she was wearing yoga pants, which meant no convenient four-way intersection of denim seams to both relieve and aggravate her excitement. Still, her inner muscles clenched, trying to create friction.

Mortified by the involuntary movement, she glanced away, hoping she could hide her reaction to his presence long enough for one of them to leave the room. Him, she decided, adjusting her computer over her lap. Men might have trouble moving about with an erection beneath their zippers, but she didn't think she'd fare much better with her knees like noodles and her head dizzying with renewed lust. Plus, her walk of shameful yearning required maneuvering stairs.

"Paige get to sleep okay?" he asked abruptly.

"Yes." Inhaling a deep breath, she touched the small gadget beside her, the size of her palm and with a single glowing green eye signaling its On status. "She has Boo with her and I found a monitor in the playroom. I set it up by her bed so now I can hear her wherever I am in the house."

"So responsible," he murmured.

Sloane sent him a sharp glance. "Is that supposed to be a criticism?"

He grunted, communicating both frustration and annoyance. "Of course not. I'm in a crap mood, is all," he said, then grimaced. "Shit mood. I'm in a shit mood."

"Are you all right?" She tried sounding like a reasonable, caring human instead of a hangry she-devil who'd rubbed against him less than twenty-four hours ago and now only wanted to do it all over again, despite knowing how unwise that would be. "Did you lose tonight?"

His laugh sounded sharp. "Yeah, in more ways than one."

"Sorry to hear that," she said, then hesitated. "Is there anything I can do?" If he asked for a bowl of ice cream, she'd have to dive head-first into the carton to cool her head and the thoughts inside it, because she kept recalling things she'd left undone last night.

The hair, she should have played more with that.

That torso. God, she wanted to lick him, from his collarbones to his belly button, with side trips along those hard abdominals. Suddenly she wondered about his nipples.

Never, not once in her life, had she considered the color or the sensitivity of a man's nipples.

Heat prickled along her scalp and she took a death grip on her laptop.

God. She was ready to eat him up in long licks and tiny bites and she hadn't even mentally made it to what he had going on beneath his jeans.

A flood of giddy, improper delight rushed through her as Sloane realized that she, a single mother and someone who'd not felt sexual in years, was having distinctly dirty thoughts.

Oh, well, she decided, tamping down on the accompanying onslaught of nerves, with Eli she was safe. They'd already hashed out the situation that morning. She'd made clear she didn't expect him to act as her...as her, um, body of convenience.

As soon as she returned to her own place and if she continued to have these...urges—doubtful, perhaps, it could be spring fever or something—she'd online order some sex toys. Satisfaction didn't require actual man parts in a complete package like Eli's, who had a gorgeous face and lean muscles, not to mention—

"I was thinking we might go to bed together," he said now. "Have actual sex."

"What?" She stared at him.

He looked back, unblinking. "I wondered if we might fuck."

"Um…" Her mind could not grasp the meaning of his words.

"Poker was a bust," he said. "I never lose like I did tonight. So then I went to Domino's—a local bar…do you know it?"

She shook her head.

"It doesn't matter." He gestured with his hand and glanced away. "I hoped to meet a woman. Somebody who'd want to have sex with me. That was a bust too."

Her eyes widened. "No woman wanted to have sex with you?" A thought struck and she felt a sudden pang of sympathy. Perhaps he'd made an embarrassing assumption. "Is Domino's a gay bar and you didn't know?"

His lips twitched. "No. It's an every-flavor-is-welcome-and-present bar, and there were plenty of women I could have approached."

Sloane wondered how that would go, exactly. "Do you just flat-out proposition them?" she asked, curious. "Or is there some protocol or code words or something?"

"I planned on offering to buy them a drink first."

"But no one was thirsty?" She still couldn't

understand how they'd gotten here. Had he actually proposed that she and he have sex?

"No one caught my eye," he said simply, his gaze meeting hers and not letting it go. "I kept thinking of you."

That's when she knew this wasn't a dream. That she wasn't actually dozing on the couch and her brain had taken itself on a fanciful holiday. Because even her Dream Lover wouldn't be so direct and sound so sincere. *I kept thinking of you.*

Wow. She gulped. "You're serious."

He lifted an eyebrow. "You're free to say no, and you can trust that I won't...bother you any further if you do."

"Of course I know that," she snapped.

"So here's the thing. It's been implied several times today that I should loosen up a little. Realize I'm twenty-nine and not seventy-nine. It occurred to me that you could use a little string-less fun, too."

String-less fun. A tingle raced down her spine and she hoped she wasn't gawking at him, because she hadn't thought about having string-less fun since she was eighteen, got her first job as a receptionist at a temp company, and blew a small chunk of her first paycheck on a new haircut at a fancy salon.

"A night of string-less sex," Eli said again. "For fun. To blow off steam. An opportunity to explore mutual pleasure. For one night."

He dangled it like a diamond bracelet.

*One night of mutual pleasure.* Her heart started to pound. "I haven't had, um, actual sex in more than four years," she confessed. "I might be no good at it."

"It's been almost twelve entire months for me," he said, "and I'd crack a joke about how long that is in dog time, but I don't feel like making you laugh right now."

She knew what he did feel like making her do, it was in that intense look in his eyes, a look that caused a rush of liquid heat through her veins. It made it hard to think, let alone talk, but he was being so direct and honest with her, she could do no less.

"Maybe I was never good at sex," she said, swallowing hard. "Paige's dad certainly didn't stick around for my sexual talents."

"Did you want to talk about that? About him?" He scooted down the sofa cushions, gathering the papers between them and setting the stack on the coffee table. Then he took away the last of her armor, her laptop, and put it aside as well. They now sat inches apart. "It's up to you."

"I..." She might as well tell Eli everything, she thought, hanging her head. "I worked for his family's large real estate office...that's where we met. I know JJ liked me right away, and he probably liked even more that me being his girlfriend would outrage his mother."

Warm fingers closed over hers. "Go on."

She breathed in, looked up. "Being his wife would be even more outrageous, right? Then his parents would see he wasn't willing to toe the familial line, go to business school, enter the family business, etcetera, etcetera."

"You wanted to be his wife?"

"I wanted the family he promised me we'd have right away. I wanted to belong to somebody. It was enough to convince me I was in love."

His hand squeezed hers. "So you got married?" At her nod, he asked. "How did his parents react?"

"It could have been worse, but Diane's mother was struggling with an Alzheimer's diagnosis, so she had more pressing worries.

"We eloped to Las Vegas and I'd got pregnant almost immediately afterward. Soon enough JJ didn't consider the whole thing such a fun jab in the eye to them anymore. He didn't see *me* as fun anymore."

Eli's thumb stroked over her knuckles. "I'm sorry, Sloane."

"Don't. I got Paige, my person to belong to," she said, lifting her chin. "But JJ died in a diving accident in Belize before she was born and I feel sorry that he lost his life running away from me and our child. I feel sorry that his parents lost their son."

"Not your fault," Eli said, squeezing her hand again. "You know that, right?"

Her nose stung and her eyes felt hot. "Most of the time, yes."

They sat in silence a few moments, and then as if he could read her need, he pulled her closer, into his arms, onto his lap. His warmth surrounded her, the closeness companionable, accepting. Perhaps platonic.

To him.

But in Eli's embrace, she didn't feel mere friendliness coursing through her bloodstream. Her nipples were beaded, her womb felt heavy. An ache persisted between her thighs. She turned her head into his throat, trying to hide her reaction. Breathing him in didn't help matters.

God, she thought she might spontaneously combust any second.

She licked her lips, and somehow her tongue managed a small taste of the slightly salty skin of his neck. Beneath her, she felt him tense. So she had to ask.

"Have I ruined the mood with all that?" She squeezed shut her eyes. "And with my four years of celibacy?"

He brushed his mouth against her hair and his arms tightened. "Not a chance. I take it as a challenge, and I like challenges."

# Chapter 8

Eli had never considered it possible to slow roll a one-night stand, but he and Sloane managed it. After her couch confession and his declaration of enjoying a challenge, he'd stood with her in his arms. She'd leaned down to scoop up the monitor and he'd appreciated her sense of responsibility—shut up, Nora—and then he'd carried her into his room. The lamp on one bedside table glowed, as did another on the table by the window that was flanked with a pair of armchairs, softly lighting the space.

Setting her on her feet, he'd asked if she'd like a glass of wine.

"Sure," she'd said, and as he stepped toward the doorway, he'd watched her drift in the direction of the attached bathroom and glance inside.

"That shower," she'd said, looking at him with wide eyes.

"You haven't seen it before?"

She'd shook her head.

"My one major home improvement, forced on me by an unfortunate plumbing leak." Upon getting the diagnosis, Boone and Hart had convinced him to pull out the big tub and the narrow stand-up stall and replace them both with a double-headed walk-in shower. The white subway and penny tile finishes didn't over-modernize the space, and he had to admit he appreciated the renovation. "Resale value," he'd said, then hesitated. "Would you like to use it?"

Her smile had told him everything, which was why, after dawdling in the kitchen, he'd come back to the bedroom to find her wrapped from throat-to-floor in his big flannel robe, her face flushed and her hair a tangle of damp curls.

He'd stared at them, fascinated. "They just do that?" he'd asked, rotating one finger over the top of his head to indicate the blonde spirals.

"They just do that," she'd confirmed, and came forward to take a glass from him. He'd put the other on the table by the windows and then had crossed to the bathroom. "I won't be long," he'd told her. "Make yourself comfortable."

Now he walked out of the steamy space dressed only in a pair of slouchy pajama pants, his own hair damp and his face freshly shaved.

From her seat on one of the armchairs, Sloane glanced over and the direction of her eyes had him ducking his chin to scrutinize his shoulders, noting a few stray drops of water. "What?" he asked her.

"One's, um, rolling down." She gestured vaguely with her wineglass, and again he followed her gaze to see the lone rivulet traveling along his pectoral muscle.

Instead of putting on a T-shirt as he'd intended, he made his way to the second chair and sat down, reaching for his own glass. He grinned, noting she hadn't looked away from his naked chest. He'd take that.

"Shall we make a toast?" he asked.

Blinking, her head lifted and now she looked at his face. "To…what?"

"'May we kiss who we please and please who we kiss,'" he said, and touched the rim of his glass to hers.

After a dutiful sip, she eyed him, her expression doubtful. "That sounded practiced. Twelve months, you say?"

He crossed his heart with one finger, watching her gaze drop there. "Truth. I don't have a lot of free time, I have four sisters, I—"

"Have a lot of excuses," she finished for him.

He blinked. "Uh..."

"You must have had a girlfriend here and there."

"Here and there." He shrugged. "But they didn't last long, no matter how well-intended, because my sisters have always come first."

Sipping from her glass, she sat back in her chair. This time she inspected him from the top of his head to his bare feet and he wondered if the heat in her gaze might cause his damp skin to start steaming. "So," she said, "I'm truly going to be the first in a while to have a chance at that buff body?"

He nearly choked on his swallow of wine.

Before he could answer she licked a drop of her own from her puffy bottom lip. "You must go to the gym a lot."

"No." He set his glass down, wondering who was in charge of this seduction. "I do a lot of lifting at work."

"Right." She placed her wine on the table as well and leaned forward, her voice going low. "It shows. In a very nice way."

The seductive tone made him want to laugh almost as much as he wanted to jump her bones. "Sloane—"

"Okay. Fine." She slumped back in her seat, looking defeated. "That's it," she said then, throwing up her hands. "I'm officially no good at this."

Laughter welled once more, which he thought was strange when his cock was taking her presence, in his robe and likely nothing else, very seriously. "What are you talking about?"

"Can't you tell?" Her arms flew up again. "I've run out of flirtatious banter."

Charmed by her, her blonde curls and her pouting mouth, not to mention her earnestness in the face of this event that he'd advertised as fun, Eli could only smile at her again. "Good," he said, then grabbed her hand and yanked her to her feet. "Because I don't want to talk anymore."

Slow rolling in poker was considered bad manners, he reminded himself.

It was a matter of seconds to pull back the covers and push her onto the bed. She landed there, the robe's tie loosening at her waist. The sides parted, gapping enough so he could see the inner curves of her impressive breasts, the tiny hollow of her navel, and the strip of gold curls leading to her sex.

Heat flashed over him. Dropping to his knees on the mattress, he peeled aside the fabric to expose all the prettiness of her, from the creamy breasts with their mauve-pink crests, to the lips of her sex, the outer ones beginning to open to expose the furled inner petals. He breathed in, smelling his soap and her arousal, and he lowered his head to place a reverent kiss on each nipple, her belly between mons and navel, then the top of the fissure that opened to her center.

Her legs moved, twitching in response and he insinuated himself between them, pushing at her inner thighs to open her wider, to open her sex, too, so he could see the moisture gathering there, in that intricate and tender arrangement of secret flesh that wasn't going to be a secret to him any longer.

"Aren't you going to kiss me?" she asked, drawing his gaze upward from her pussy.

"I'm definitely going to kiss you," he said, then arranged himself so that her thighs went over his shoulders and he could settle in on his elbows, his raging cock momentarily mollified by pressing it against the sheets.

Sloane's hand came to his head, fingers curling in his hair. "Not…there? No one's kissed me there."

He glanced up again, taking in her flushed face and the darkness of her eyes, pupils eclipsing the irises. "Then definitely there," he said, and lowered his head. Ignoring her little protest, he breathed deep then kissed her, his mouth open and his tongue out, giving her suction and swirl, tasting her and taking the honey inside. Swallowing the sweetness made his belly tighten and his cock reflexively dig into the cotton beneath it.

Her clutching hand was no longer pulling, but it tightened for a second then fell to the mattress in surrender. Sweet, swift surrender.

He applied himself to her pleasure and to his discovery, licking soft surfaces and glancing off the small hard one. She tilted her pelvis, offering up her clit, but he avoided it then, sliding down and then into her tight channel, forcing his stiff tongue as far as it could go, breaking into a sweat as he tasted another flood of her desire.

His hand crept up her hip and her ribs to her breast. And he thumbed the nipple, feeling her body begin to hum. Her hips tilted again, a sharper angle, and he buried his face in her juicy pussy, wanting her scent all over him, committing this one-night stand to sensual memory.

He was lost in everything Sloane when the crisis crashed over her. "Oh!" she cried out, her hands clawing at the sheets, her body arching. He slid his mouth to her clit and pushed a long finger inside her. As she began to quake, he sucked her nub and drove into her slick channel, again and again, now with two fingers, feeling her close over them with muscles contracting furiously.

As the climax receded, he gentled his mouth and slid his fingers free. Resting the side of his head on the pillow of her thigh, he lapped at her with soothing strokes. When she'd quieted completely, he sat up and brought his wet fingers to his mouth, sucking her release from them.

He met her eyes, shrugged. "You taste…"

"What?" she asked, going from sated-looking to curious.

"Like this," he answered, then crawled over her to kiss her, sliding his tongue against hers, tasting her deeply so she could taste herself just as thoroughly.

She moaned and her hands came up to his shoulders. Digging in, she kneaded him like a cat, pressing her lips to his, totally immersed in the kiss.

As he backed away, she rose up on her elbows to maintain the connection, and he chuckled, the sound muffled by her demanding mouth. When he tore free of her, she looked on him with a ridiculously adorable yet addled expression on her face. A woman in afterglow. Something moved in his chest—his heart, rolling over.

Before he could think to worry over it, Sloane had jackknifed up and now launched herself at him, taking him down to his back, with her hovering over him in a tangle of heated limbs and inconvenient flannel. Between them, they struggled with the material, and once it was wrenched free, she leaned down to his mouth and planted a searing kiss there. But it was a quick kiss, because she was already on the move, her tongue flattening to draw a wet line over his jaw and down his throat. She traced his collarbones with it and he sifted his fingers in her curls as she bumped over his nipple.

It tightened to a sharp point and he groaned, holding her head as she explored the sensitive tip, torturing him with different techniques from lashing to lapping. Then she sucked, causing his hips to buck. Her sharp little teeth were employed next and lightning whipped through his body, pre-cum spurting from the crown of his cock.

His hand flew down, squeezing to keep control of the orgasm churning in his balls. She gave his nipple a last, soothing lick, then played games with the other one, as he thought of cold climates and cold showers and cold shoulders, anything to keep from coming too soon.

Her gaze caught his and he was struck by the light in her eyes, mischief and power and something so feminine it gave him pause. "Sloane," he said as a warning, because trouble was brewing.

She slid down, her fingers hooking in the waistband of his pajama pants. "*Shh*," she said, easing them down. "I'll be gentle."

On a groan, his head tilted back, into the pillow, and he lifted his hips so she could work the cotton lower. His knees cocked open as she pulled the fabric free and she accepted his invitation, coming into the space he'd made for her. Licking the hard-on that was all for her.

Maybe no one had ever gone down on her, but she gave head like she enjoyed it, humming as she took him into her mouth, her little tongue circling and tickling, poking into the slit at the crown to lick up the liquid welling there. He groaned, his muscles twitching then tensing, his balls drawing tighter. Blindly he reached for the drawer in the bedside table.

Condom, he thought, desperate to get inside her before he lost control.

A packet finally grasped, he tore it open with his teeth, then gently drew her away from his cock, his fingers wrapped in those curls of hers. Donning the condom was clumsy work with shaking hands, and she finally took over, rolling it over him.

Then he brought her down and rolled on top of her, adjusted. He reminded himself to take it slow and shallow, it had been a long time for both of them.

Four years for her.

Twelve months for him.

He was shaking again, all over, as he fitted the

head to her pussy and slid along the wet flesh until he could push in, breaching her with just the crown. She gasped and he kissed her, a soft kiss, a lover's kiss. Not a one-night stand kiss.

But he didn't think of that as he drove in another inch. Her arms went around his neck and her hips tilted to take more. To take him, a lover, her lover.

He began to thrust now, he couldn't bear not to, and she was with him, little moans leaking from where their two pairs of lips joined, and the soft sounds were what did him in. He drove harder and her head fell back, denting the pillow. He bit her chin and sucked on the side of her neck, as he slid his hand down between their bodies to find her clit.

She shivered and he felt it in his dick and there, there it was. Her climax shuddered through her body as she cried out. In response, pleasure eddied in his balls and then rushed up his shaft. He lunged into her channel once more, taking her with a rough thrust, but she responded to it, her body bucking upward as semen shot from him, so much seed he worried he'd overflow the latex.

So much sensation, he worried about ever having the will to leave Sloane, now going lax against him.

But he did, moving quickly so as not to spill a drop, because he would never want to put a woman at risk.

When he came back to the bed she was out. Gone to the world. He moved her boneless body, marveling at the heaviness of her small limbs, post-coitus. When she was satisfactorily positioned, he wound himself around her. His mental alarm clock was in perfect working order.

He set it for sixty minutes of sleep.

One night was all they had and after a recharge he hoped she'd be ready for more.

Sloane helped sleepy-eyed Paige into her clothes, with Boo looking on with less patience. He knew the drill. Once her daughter was up and dressed, he'd get a walk before breakfast. "Did you have a good sleep, Mama?" Paige asked, mimicking her mother's first words of the day.

"Thank you, baby, I did." As the little girl wrestled with the pair of socks she handed her, Sloane smoothed the bedclothes, finding Baby Sally under a pillow and pulling her out to save her from a day of smothering beneath down feathers.

With her small team finally ready, she took Paige by the hand and headed downstairs. "Shh," she told her daughter, finger to her lips. "Eli is still sleeping."

Eli had been sleeping when she'd decided to leave his bed an hour before dawn too. Despite the monitor on the table near her pillow, she'd wanted to wait out her daughter's awakening in her own room. The man had roused as she stirred, and at her quick explanation he'd merely leaned up to kiss her cheek.

An affectionate gesture, she'd thought. Warm. Almost like something a father might bestow on a mother when it was her turn to get up with the crying infant.

A ridiculous notion, she decided now, scowling. It made zero sense to think of him in those terms, not when their string-less night was over.

But it was no time for frowns either, she admonished herself, ushering Paige into the kitchen so she could down a half-cup of coffee before their walk. Last night had been everything he'd promised. A way to blow off steam. An opportunity to explore mutual pleasure. Fun.

Without any expectations of it happening again with Eli or with anyone else, for that matter, she was going to hold the memory close. Maybe even savor it a little. More than a little.

"Let's go," she said to Boo, clicking the spring hook on the leash. He ran over, a huge grin on his face. Happy with the prospect of Now.

An example for her. She latched him up and he pranced to the front door, Paige trailing. The little physical twinges Sloane felt between her thighs only served to remind her that she'd had a great time in bed with the man—and that she didn't have to spend every hour of her life considering consequences and forecasting the future in order to pre-plan for all eventualities.

Last night, she'd lived in the moment.

Today she was going to do the same.

The spring morning tasted fresh on her tongue and already the sun warmed the air and sparkled on the dew dotting the tree leaves and long grasses along the side of the road. Per Boo's choice, they turned away from both Eli's house and her own, and she let him dictate the speed and rate of stopping and going.

Which meant they ambled along and often took breaks so he could sniff and water telephone poles and sprouting dandelions. Neighboring houses were few and set back from the road and though it was Friday, apparently no one was in a hurry to get to work.

Sloane lifted her face to the sun and let the rays wash over her. This living for the moment business had a lot to recommend itself. Her office was closed Fridays and Eli had mentioned it was his day off from the nursery…meaning they might bump into each other at the house more than normal.

But she wasn't going to turn that into a cause for concern. She and her small posse had reached a utility box that served as their turnaround point, and Boo circled it and then headed back in the direction they'd come. "Would you like pancakes for breakfast?" Sloane asked Paige, who was trailing a long stick across the bumpy asphalt.

The little girl stopped, her downy brows coming together. "Blueberry syrup?"

"I'm pretty sure we have some." She'd brought a box of varied foodstuffs from her house.

"Yay!" Her doubts alleviated, Paige jumped up and down with enthusiasm.

Sloane smiled, heart going even lighter at her daughter's appreciation of such a simple thing. It's what she'd wanted for her from the day the home test showed positive, it's what she worked for every hour. Paige didn't need to be raised with luxuries, but Sloane believed a strong foundation of love and blueberry syrup would instill a confidence that would make her daughter into a good person who could live a positive life.

Maybe too heavy a thought for such a lovely morning. Sloane laughed at herself and began skipping, a skill she'd recently taught Paige. Her daughter imitated her movements, and Boo frisked at their side as they made their way to Eli's.

She'd cook enough pancakes for him, she decided, and leave them warming in the oven in case he chose to sleep late. Bacon, too, because he'd probably be hungry.

A grin overtook her face. After all, he'd expended a lot of calories the night before.

Up ahead, a car appeared. Automatically Sloane ushered the dog and Paige toward the edge of the road. Sidewalks would make the lane safer, but it would take away from the rural atmosphere.

"Paige," she warned, as she saw the car slow near her own small cottage. "Closer to the side, please. Stay right in front of me."

Her hand on her daughter's shoulder, she saw the vehicle stop. A woman emerged from the driver's side, then waved.

"Oh." Sloane's mood dimmed as she recognized JJ's sister. The other woman, in her late-thirties, looked as put-together as always, her dark hair in a sleek fall of layers. "There's Aunt Rona."

Though Boo had already started up Eli's driveway, Sloane tugged on the leash to return him to the road. Paige looked curiously at the other woman, then back at her mom. "Aunt Rona," she repeated, as if the name was only vaguely familiar.

Guilt pinched Sloane. Though they'd not seen JJ's sister in almost four months, since Paige's grandparents had last visited California, she should probably talk about the woman more. Surely she had some photos of her to show her daughter. They could call her on the phone.

"Let's go say hi," she said, urging Paige forward. The other woman ran her gaze over Sloane, from her tumbled hair to the ragged sneakers she was wearing with ankle-length jeans and her Duffy's T-shirt. In the shower that morning she'd found bruises on her inner thighs and one on the skin inside her hip. Then, she'd considered them symbols of a night well spent, but they began to throb now, and she hoped Rona couldn't detect the heat rising on her face.

Once they were within earshot, JJ's sister took another quick peruse of her. "Sloane," Rona said. "You look…comfortable."

The implied criticism reminded her of just why she didn't pursue the relationship, though her disapproval was merely a pale reflection of her mother Diane's. Still, Sloane tacked on a smile. "What a surprise," she said. "What are you doing here?"

"I had an early meeting in Sawyer Beach." Rona brushed a piece of unseen lint off her sleeve. She owned a successful, high-end advertising firm in San Luis Obispo, which meant one of their local businesses must be sinking some big bucks into promotion.

"It was so nice of you to stop by," Sloane said. "Could you come in…" The words spilled from her mouth before she could stop them. She'd have to renege on the offer, she thought in a sudden panic. Somehow explain that her home was for all intents and purposes condemned. Her stomach roiled, knowing she'd feel exposed and disgraced, no matter that it wasn't her fault.

Rona, thank goodness, shook her head. "I don't have time for a visit," she said.

Sloane worked against sagging in relief.

"But I brought something for Paige." Leaning into her car, she pulled out a pink-and-yellow, shrink-wrapped Easter basket. "Here," she said, addressing the little girl for the first time. "This is for you."

"How nice," Sloane said, helping place the item in her daughter's arms. More guilt stung. Maybe she could have turned to Rona when she had a housing emergency. Alice and Joe were still not answering their phones. "Say thank you, Paige."

"Thank you," the child dutifully parroted, peering through the plastic covering at the candy and plastic toys.

Intrigued by the basket, Boo reared up to inspect it, getting close to Rona.

"Bad dog," the woman scolded, stepping back. "Shedding hair all over." She brushed at her skirt.

Sloane choked up on the leash, bringing the dog nearer and giving him a consoling rub with her knee. Rona didn't like pets, she recalled now. So no, Paige's aunt wasn't going to be taking in Sloane's little family.

Still, she had made a special trip to see her niece. "I hope you can come to Paige's birthday party," Sloane said. "I'll be sure to email you an invitation. It's scheduled for the Saturday before Easter."

Thank goodness she'd planned to hold it at a local park, and not her own cottage. A few of Paige's daycare friends and parents made up the guest list, and a handful of others, along with Alice and Joe who expected to be back from their road trip.

"I'm gonna be four," Paige piped up.

"Yes," Rona said, looking at the little girl, then addressing Sloane. "Mother already told me about the party. I think I can make it."

"Oh." Diane was passing out invitations now? Tamping down her irritation, Sloane put on another smile. "It would be great to have you there, your husband as well. I know your parents would enjoy it too."

"About that..."

The unfamiliar note in the brunette's voice felt like a cold fingernail along Sloane's spine. She glanced up at the blue sky and felt warmth on her face again. Sun, fresh air, her daughter and her dog by her side, she reminded herself. *Live in the moment!*

"Sloane, you know Mom and Dad are planning on staying in Sawyer Beach when they arrive next week."

"Yes. I'm sure you're disappointed—"

"This is my mother we're talking about," Rona said, a more human ruefulness infusing the tone of her voice. "I live in their former house. Do you suppose I keep it up to her standards?"

Sloane felt a rush of sympathy. Diane's displeasure with her son's wife took the form of pinched lips and semi-veiled criticisms. She likely didn't censor herself to that extent with her daughter.

"Last visit," Rona continued, "she told me I needed a new vacuum cleaner. I'm almost forty years old and my mother instructs me when to buy a home appliance."

Sloane grimaced. Yes, maybe the mainly silent censure wasn't so bad. "I'm sure that's disheartening, Rona."

"It's nothing compared to what she has in mind for you," the other woman said bluntly.

Sloane froze. "What?" she managed to choke out.

"I don't want to frighten you…or maybe I think you should be frightened."

"Paige," Sloane said, urgent. Every instinct inside her alerted, and adrenaline shot through her bloodstream, her body priming for danger. "Take your new basket and go sit on the front steps." With a shaking finger, she pointed toward their cottage. "I need just a minute to speak with your aunt."

Paige complied, and Sloane kept her gaze on her daughter until she'd taken a seat on the concrete as directed. Then she steeled herself and turned toward the other woman. "Rona, what are you talking about?"

"It's what my mother's talking about that is concerning me. That will concern you." She inhaled a deep breath and her dark eyes didn't leave Sloane's. "She wants Paige. She's talking about getting custody of her, full-time custody, and taking her to live with her and my dad in Florida."

# Chapter 9

Though the nursery's posted schedule showed Friday to be a day off for Eli, as he shoved back the covers on his bed he decided to go into work anyway. In the kitchen, he noted the brewed carafe of coffee and Boo's missing leash and surmised that Sloane and company were on a morning walk.

As he grabbed the keys to his truck, he considered leaving a note but then decided against the idea.

Their night was over. It wasn't fair or wise to do anything that she might misconstrue as an attempt to extend their connection.

String-less sex was what he'd offered, what she'd agreed to, all that he'd recall when he cast his mind back to those hours in his dimly lit bedroom, when he'd touched and kissed and tasted her everywhere. When she'd responded with a gratifying delight and embarked on her own fair share of exploration of his body with a sweet enthusiasm.

He closed his eyes for a moment, then gripped the keys, the slight pain of the sharp edges yanking him back to the present.

To his real life, the rambling house that would soon be much too big for a carefree bachelor, to the business that he sweated over because it was the King legacy and also work that he very much enjoyed, to the future waiting in the near-distance that promised him a new and very welcome independence.

The drive to King's took little time at this early hour and he eschewed taking a seat behind his desk to walk about the grounds, pitching in where he saw that a pair of extra hands could prove useful. He slung bags of brown mulch for the weekend special display, unboxed pump bottles of indoor plant food, and swept up shards of a large earthenware pot taken out by a too-sharp turn of a forklift.

Once he'd used raw muscle power to rearrange two-dozen ten-gallon potted shrubs, he decided he deserved a coffee break and made himself a cup in the break room. Then he dropped into his desk chair, the activities of the night before pushed to the farther reaches of his mind.

He was entering numbers in a spreadsheet on his computer screen when a knock on his doorjamb made him glance up.

"Hey, Boone." The big man lingered in the doorway. "What's up?"

"You busy?"

"It's my day off, so I shouldn't even be here."

Boone dropped into one of the visitors' chairs. "I was in the area, so I thought I'd take a chance on finding you. Though I wondered if you might be too worn out to make it into work today."

Eli steeled himself against reacting to his friend's assessing gaze. "Here I am," he said, holding his hands out to his sides. "What did you need?"

"It's what you missed by leaving poker early last night," he said, and lifted onto one hip to withdraw something from his back pocket. "You owe me twenty bucks."

Though Eli's eyebrows rose, he automatically reached into his own pocket for his wallet. "What is it I purchased?"

"Raffle tickets. Maddox is selling them. Some fund-raiser being sponsored by the local police department."

Eli handed over a twenty-dollar bill and received four tickets in return. He glanced at them. "And I'll win…"

"There are lots of possibilities, little to big. But don't hold your breath for the grand prize. You know who's going to take that."

"Cooper," they said together. Though the man didn't generally clean up on poker night, at any other contest, especially those that required luck over skill, their friend came out on top more than his fair share of the time. He was the guy who found a fifty in the gutter. The one who pulled into the last available parking spot in their favorite beachside lot.

Boone shook his head. "One of these days he's going to lose out on something he really wants."

"It'll knock him on his ass."

Speaking of which…" Boone narrowed his eyes. "You look like you're dragging."

A second mention of his obvious fatigue. Eli

scraped his hand through his hair and downed more coffee.

Boone wasn't put off. "Successful night?"

"Maybe we can go out for margaritas or sangria after our next hair appointments and dish."

"Don't try going sexist on me, asshole," his friend said, scowling. "As a brother of four young women you should be ashamed of yourself."

Eli ignored the swipe, but felt guilty all the same. And Christ, he'd brought the question on himself, after all, by bellyaching about his needs to the poker crew.

"Look," he said. "I'm pleasantly worn out from my exertions last night. Is that enough to get you off my back?"

"Only if you give me a little hint about the identity of the fortunate woman." At Eli's stare, Boone shrugged. "Okay, I admit I made a little side bet with myself. Do I owe me ten bucks because you bumped uglies with your neighbor-now-roomie?"

"Shut. Up," Eli said. "Nothing about Sloane is ugly."

Boone started to laugh. "I'm sorry. That *was* rude." Then he made a big show of drawing out his wallet again, taking a ten from it, then slipping the bill back inside.

Watching the performance, Eli sighed. "Keep it to yourself, okay?"

"Not another word…except, is this a one and done or are you two started something more serious?"

Eli recoiled. "You know I've been serious for the last eleven years. That's not what I want now."

"One and done, then." Boone sat back in his chair.

"Yes. We talked about it last night. Before."

But after, meaning after the three times he'd come and the four times for her, had they talked at all? No, they'd passed out in each other's arms until she'd slipped from the bed at dawn. Later, he'd used her absence from the house to escape to work and who knew what she was thinking now...or what she was thinking he was thinking now.

Crap.

He put his elbow on his desk and propped his forehead on the heel of his hand. "I should have left a note," he muttered. "Or flowers. Should I have sent flowers?"

"Nope," Boone said, adamant. "You said you discussed it beforehand. One and done. You're covered, bro. Flowers would only confuse things."

Eli looked up. "Somehow this seems wrong. I'm relying on you for romantic advice?"

The big man stood, and that had to be a smirk on his face. "Romantic? Who used that word?"

Then he left, his whistle loud in the hallway.

His words loud in Eli's head. Right. Nothing about last night had been romantic. It wasn't supposed to be. But he could have been more considerate this morning. At the very least made sure he set his eyes on the woman.

Scooping his phone off the desk, he rose and headed for the exit, driven by a new urge. He needed to check on Sloane. In person.

The car ride took longer than he liked, as he had to travel through the Sawyer Beach downtown with its Friday noontime traffic. It gave him time to replay the night before and now it wasn't the sexual parts that rolled through his head. He remembered Sloane sharing the particulars about her marriage.

*I wanted to belong to somebody.*

He hated how alone she'd been. How vulnerable that had made her when she was so young.

*He didn't see* me *as fun anymore.*

And then to be betrayed by the person who'd promised her a place in the world by his side. Dead or not, Eli wanted to punch the guy in the face. Paige's father hadn't deserved his daughter or his wife.

As he pulled into the garage, he was glad that he still lived in the old place at the moment. It was there to provide a roof over the head of his neighbor and her child. Pushing through the door from the garage into the kitchen, he met the gaze of the woman in question. "Hey," he said, taking in her rumpled curls and the flannel shirt she wore, the tails hanging down to her knees and revealing bare legs and bare feet covered by slouchy socks. She could wear a burlap sack and he'd find her sexy as hell. He put one hand on the wall to steady himself as he recalled the sweet, molten heat of her kiss. "Sloane—"

"Eli," she said, her voice urgent. "Go away."

"What?" He rocked back on one heel, wondering if he'd been clumsy in bed the night before in some way he hadn't perceived. Had he hurt her physically? But no, he didn't believe that. Yeah, she'd been tight because it had been a long period of abstinence for her. And yeah, he'd not been the gentlest of lovers 100 percent of the time. But she'd arched her back as he'd nipped the tight crests of her breasts and her heels had dug into his ass with every rough thrust into her body. Perhaps she'd been a little sore upon awakening, but her moans and clutching hands while in the throes of climax were evidence she'd thoroughly enjoyed the source of any aches and pains.

Then had his absence that morning offended her?

He grimaced. "Look, Sloane, I'm sorry if—"

The wail of a child interrupted his apology and Sloane spun and dashed for the stairs. He followed, galvanized by the cry.

In the doorway to Paige's room, Sloane turned to face him again and stretched her arms from jamb to jamb. "You don't want to catch this. Stomach flu."

Ah. He hovered in the hall as she sprinted toward her daughter. Then he moved back as she rushed the child to the bathroom, the dog at her heels.

Familiar sounds confirmed the situation.

Glancing into the room, he saw a jumble of linens on the floor and Baby Sally, facedown and wearing a hand towel like a toga. He gathered up the discarded material and retrieved the doll, propping her up on a pillow.

"I'm going, I'm going," he said to the toy's accusing stare, and took the bundle of cloth in the direction of the stairs. He met Sloane coming out of the bathroom with Paige curled in her arms, the child's wan face pressed to her mother's chest. "What do you need?" he asked, unable to help himself from running a gentle hand over the little girl's silky blonde hair. "I'm here now."

Big-eyed, Sloane mutely shook her head, and sidestepped him for the bedroom.

But this wasn't Eli's first rodeo. He filled and started the washing machine, then carted a tray upstairs that held a mug of tea of for Sloane, a cup of cool water for Paige, a sleeve of soda crackers, and a short, cold bottle of cola. "When you think she can keep it down," he told the girl's mother as he set it on the dresser. "Just call if you need anything else."

She merely shook her head at him again, but did murmur "thank you" when he handed her the ignominiously named "Barf Bowl" that he'd unearthed from a back cupboard.

Paige looked at him through listless eyes. "You'll feel better," he promised. "And when you do, we'll set up Camp Movies downstairs. We show only the best there."

He prepared for the eventuality by hooking up an old DVD player he'd never got around to throwing out to the very new, very big flat-screen TV in the family room. It took some head-scratching to realize what inputs he had to use, but he got it working. The DVDs of his sisters' favorite movies were still stored in a lower cupboard. He studied the hoard in some dismay, realizing it was indicative of every nook and cranny of the old house—stashed with years upon years of King flotsam and jetsam.

It was going to be a hell of a chore to clear out before selling.

But when mother, daughter, and dog came down the stairs a couple of hours later, he was glad that he still had the movies and the player around. He and Sloane made a bed for Paige on the couch and she snuggled into one corner, with Baby Sally and a doll-size hairbrush and a tiny bucket of mini hair accessories. Sloane took to the other corner once the little girl had made her first movie selection.

To act as technical support, he sat on the floor with Boo, his back propped by the couch near Paige's corner. Soon she was entranced by the under-the-sea antics of the characters on the screen and Eli was in a semi-doze as well, barely noticing as little fingers began playing with his hair, the lack of sleep catching up with him.

"Uh, Eli…"

He twitched, jolting into alertness and turned his head to look at Sloane.

Her big blue eyes were filled with gentle amusement and he realized Paige had adorned the long strands of his hair with some of her accessory collection. He glanced at the child and saw that her color had returned and that she looked contented, hairbrush in hand, attention on the big screen.

His gaze returned to Sloane and she smiled at him. He took it like a punch to the chest as he remembered her looking that same way the night before, between Rounds one and two, with her hands stacked on his chest and her chin on her hands. She'd been rattling on about her plans for Paige's upcoming birthday party—apparently orgasming revved the woman—and he'd been trying to believe his cock hadn't been permanently incapacitated after his last explosive climax.

*Oh, but what a way to go,* he'd thought, and then had gotten it up again in less than an hour.

"Eli," she said now, nodding toward him. "Shall I get her to take those out—"

"No. It's nothing that's not happened before," he said, reaching up to touch the little pieces of plastic dangling from the ends of his hair. "Don't worry about it."

Being used as a hair model was indeed something he'd experienced in the past. But one thing was new, he realized as his housemate continued to gaze upon him with that soft light in her eyes.

He'd assumed he and Sloane could go back to

their previous non-relationship after last night. But seeing that smile on her face and that expression in her eyes meant she couldn't be some anonymous hookup to him. Not after spending time in his bed and not after she'd seen him at his most vulnerable—with glitter clips hanging in his hair.

At best he might manage to label her an intimate stranger.

And even that seemed like a worry worthy of some future sleepless nights.

The next afternoon, Eli arrived home from work in the early afternoon. Sloane expressed surprise— spring, weekend, a beautiful day that would turn people's thoughts to their landscaping needs—and though he waved off her comment, telling her the nursery ran like clockwork without him, she couldn't help but wonder if he'd returned to check on how she and Paige were faring.

Yesterday, he'd been on hand to help alleviate her daughter's misery. As Sloane deep-cleaned the kitchen, she smiled, remembering the way he'd looked with half a dozen barrettes affixed to the ends of his hair. At one point he'd even been humming along with the movie playing on the TV and with a single look at Paige she'd diagnosed a growing case of hero worship.

Much better than the stomach flu, she'd decided then. Now it was the reason she allowed the little girl to play nearby while he tackled the chore of uncluttering and organizing his garage.

He said he didn't mind and Sloane trusted him.

But the quiet inside the house gave her too much time with her own thoughts. With a last swipe of the interior of the refrigerator, she put together a tray of lemonade and graham crackers. Rona's warning about Diane and Jeffrey seeking custody had been lost in the haze of Paige's sudden attack of stomach distress. But now the concern was bubbling up again, and Sloane felt helpless to control it—as well as helpless to take a positive action against the threat.

Maybe it was all talk. Maybe Rona had overheard something her mother said and taken the words out of context.

So Sloane decided against borrowing trouble. As a single parent, working paycheck to paycheck, there were only so many worries she could juggle at one time. Until this one presented itself more credibly, she refused to let it bring down her mood.

For the moment, her daughter's health had improved, the sun was shining, and in less than a week her landlords would have returned and they would help her get back into her own home. She shouldered her way out the kitchen door and into the garage.

Until then, this nice man was sharing his home with them.

As she stepped onto the concrete floor, and caught a glimpse of Eli, she had to admit that "nice" didn't cover it.

Neither did a shirt.

Wearing work boots, jeans, and nothing else, he was reaching for a box stacked on one of the high shelves running along the walls. The muscles in his back shifted under the surface of his sleek skin. She recalled running her hands over that same living surface as the heat and power of him slid between her thighs. Her body clenched in memory, reigniting the ache he'd left behind. He'd been big, and he'd worked slowly to enter her at first, his voice gentle. Soothing. *Relax baby, you can take me. God, how wet you are, how ready for me.*

It was she who'd gone crazy at the sensation of being filled with such heat and girth, desire shooting through her bloodstream, need making her clutch and suck and kiss with increasing demand.

Knees going wobbly, she set down her tray on the work bench just as he hefted the box in his arms and then bent to set it on the floor. As he glanced over at her, Sloane grabbed up a napkin and fanned her face. "Such a warm day," she said, hoping to excuse her blush.

Eli gave her a longer look, then redirected his attention to the cardboard flaps, opening them. "Paige," he called out. "I found the sidewalk chalk."

Sloane's daughter skipped over and bent as well to peer inside the box. Boo joined them, and she had to grin at the three heads so close together. Paige reached inside and brought up two thick pieces of chalk, one pink and one blue.

"What are you going to draw?" he asked the little girl as they both straightened.

"You and me," she said. "Boo too."

"I like it." He smiled. "The driveway is all yours, but stay away from the street, okay?"

"Okay." She whirled in that direction, then whirled back. "You smell."

"Uh-oh," With a grimace, he lifted one arm and made an elaborate sniff. "Bad?"

"Like a daddy," she said. "My friend Jace has two

daddies. I like daddies."

"Ah."

She started off again, then glanced over her shoulder. "I like you."

"Back your way, kid." Eli took the offering with a coolness Sloane didn't feel. "And I'm honored."

She inhaled a quick breath when he shifted his gaze to her. "Well," she said, trying conceal the emotion she felt at further proof of her daughter's first crush. "As you can see, the director of Camp Movies made quite an impression."

Turning toward the work bench, she poured a glass of lemonade and held it out. "You must be thirsty." He ventured nearer, and, like Paige, now she could smell that intoxicating scent of his. Clean soap with just an edge of lime. His robe had smelled of it. His chest. His belly.

He took the glass and shook his head. "I can't believe I kept a box of half-used sidewalk chalk."

"But it came in handy," she pointed out.

"The people who buy this house next likely won't think so. It's all going to have to go." He sighed, then tipped his head back for a long swallow of the icy beverage.

She averted her eyes from his throat, tanned and strong-looking. It's possible she wanted to bite it. "I'm not sure I thanked you for your help with Paige yesterday. I could have handled it by myself…but it was good of you."

Eli shrugged. "Everybody needs help now and again."

"You raised four sisters alone."

"It wasn't easy, especially at first."

"I suppose not." She imagined him, a teenager,

dealing with his own grief and then trying to keep a household running for four grieving little girls. More welling of emotion had her turning away again to pour herself a glass. "How did you manage?"

A long silence followed. She thought he'd ignore her question until he began speaking again, his voice low.

"I used to climb up on the roof," he said. "Stupid, now that I think about it. Dangerous. But I'd go up there at night when the girls were asleep and talk to my parents."

Just talk? she wondered, glancing at him over her shoulder.

He was inspecting the surface of his lemonade as if he found it fascinating. "To tell the truth, I silent-screamed at the stars on many, many nights."

Had he read her mind? "But of course you did," she said, facing him, though she wanted to hold him more than anything—because as he stepped into his parents' shoes who had provided him comfort? "Anyone would be filled with…"

"Sadness and doubt and a heap of anger thrown in," Eli said. He drained his lemonade. "Then I felt guilty about being mad."

"For a long time I was mad at JJ too," Sloane confessed, "even though by the time of his death I knew our marriage wasn't going to survive. I was furious that Paige wasn't going to know her father—however that may have turned out."

Eli set his glass on the workbench and crossed to one of the other boxes littering the floor of the garage. He'd pulled out his truck to make room for random piles and short stacks.

He took the top off one carton and peered inside.

"These are old pairs of soccer shoes. What was I thinking?"

She watched him move about as he expressed varying degrees of dismay at the household items that had been gathering dust. "Okay, *this* is on my dad," he said, gesturing to indicate a jumble of bungee cords, coiled and twisted together like snakes in a nest. "He'd find these in a parking lot, on the street, wherever, and bring them home."

"They're useful."

He gestured to an entire stack of boxes, four-high. "All bungee cords."

"Oh." She sipped her drink, smiling a little while trying to picture the man who'd collected them.

Eli sighed. "Maybe I can hand them out next Halloween along with the candy. Probably some of them can prove useful at the nursery."

Mention of the nursery made her wonder. "Would you have done anything different if your parents had lived?" Sloane asked, then cringed at the sound of her own curiosity. "Sorry."

With two broken lampshades in hand, he glanced over. "It's okay." He tossed the items onto a pile clearly designated as rubbish. "I was headed for college to study business."

"With the intention of coming back to work at the nursery after graduation?"

"Definitely." He grinned. "But not before some skipping of class, foolish carousing, and taking exams through raging hangovers. I suppose I'm better without that experience."

Experience was what he was after now, though. "Do you ever wonder if some coed you missed meeting in the cafeteria line might have been the love of your life?"

His face turned serious. "My friend Hart Sawyer dated a girl in college. They re-met at a college reunion last year and became engaged. She died of an aneurism not long ago, right before their wedding."

"I'm so sorry." Sloane hand crept to cover her mouth.

He looked away. "So maybe it's good I didn't meet that coed either."

"Right."

As he bent to rummage through yet another box, her attention caught on something trailing from the broken zipper of a garment bag. Suede. Embroidery. With careful hands, she extricated a garment from the plastic covering. A long coat, made of square and rectangular patches of velvety leather, all of it embroidered with flowers in colorful wool strands.

Sloane couldn't help herself. She slipped her hands through the sleeves and the hem of it nearly swept her ankles. Spinning this way and that, she admired how it flared around her calves.

"That was my mother's."

Freezing midturn, her gaze flew to Eli's. Her fingers clutched at the lapels to push off the coat. "I'm sorry, I—"

"Leave it on. I like the way it looks on you."

"No." She shrugged out of the heavy suede and took care to reinsert it in the garment bag. "You should see if one of your sisters wants the coat. Don't throw it out or give it away to just anyone. It's special."

Still without looking at him, she folded the plastic in half and set it on one corner of the workbench. "What were they like together...your parents?"

Glancing over, she saw him move an old television set, boxy and heavy-looking to the discard pile. "Not a matched pair," he said.

"Oh?"

"For example, Dad loved to watch game shows on TV. Mom put her fingers in her ears when she walked through a room when one was playing."

"What was her preference?"

"Mysteries, family dramas. She denied it, but she had a soft spot for those teenage soap operas."

"So they didn't watch TV together."

"Not usually. But she worked part-time at the nursery so still they spent a lot of time with each other."

She sighed. "They were a happy couple."

He glanced over, his look sharp, his voice sharper. "They were just people. A normal couple."

Her eyes rounded. "Not happy then?"

Silence stretched. Then Eli shook his head. "No. They were happy. I only…it wasn't…well, you know how it ended."

"But all that came before…" Sloane glanced around at the evidence of a full life—the suede coat, the old TV, the dusty artificial Christmas tree in the corner, boxes of bungee cords.

"You're going to want what they had," she said, even if he put it all in the rubbish pile, she was certain of that. "And you'll find it."

His silence lingered longer this time.

The garage turned airless and Sloane's chest tightened. She'd managed to set aside Rona's warning from yesterday. But this…right now she tasted a panic impossible to ignore. "*Somebody* gets to have that," she said, her voice plaintive.

Before he came up with any kind of reply, Paige rushed in and the moment was lost.

The opportunity to hear the answer Sloane had wanted was lost too.

# Chapter 10

Sundays at the nursery usually wore Eli ragged, and this one was no exception. At six, he climbed into his truck and pointed it toward home, with a brief stop to pick up a pizza that he'd ordered while still at his desk. Without knowing what Sloane and Paige might like as toppings, he'd requested half pepperoni and half cheese, the old King family standby.

Of course, he could have called or texted to ask what the two preferred, but that smacked of...something he was avoiding. He accepted that he was regarding Sloane as more than a mere housemate. In his mind he'd settled on the term "intimate stranger," and knowing her pizza order landed too much on the side of intimacy.

Not enough on the unfamiliar.

Not enough on the here-but-would-be-gone-from-his-life-very-soon.

Pulling up to the house, he noted her missing car. He felt a pang of disquiet…or was it disappointment? Ignoring the sensation, he spied Baby Sally upended and abandoned on the porch steps and felt sure that was evidence his guests were only temporarily away.

Bowing to impulse, he braked his truck in the driveway and strode for the doll, then scooped her up. Her staring eyes sent a shiver creeping down his spine. Steeling himself, he met her gaze. "I could have left you on your head, you know," he said, straightening her sailor suit with a no-nonsense tug. Once again, one of his dress socks perched atop her messy mane of hair. He yanked it free to untangle her locks with his fingers and the scent of Sloane floated into the air.

He froze, breathing in the light and flowery notes. Her shampoo, he decided. Paige must have washed the doll's hair with her mother's brand.

In his mind's eye, he saw his fingers buried in her blonde curls, holding her head steady for a deep, ravishing kiss. He nearly groaned, recalling how she'd slid her small tongue against his as their naked bodies lay entwined, their legs tangled so that his hard cock surged against her thigh and the melting heat and wet of her pussy pressed against his.

*Hell.*

Pushing away the sensual memories the scent had invoked, he sat Baby Sally by the front door then backed slowly away. Two gulps of fresh air cleared his head and he jogged to the driver's side of his truck, deciding a little more distance was required.

He wasn't supposed to be dwelling on their night together.

*One and done.*

Without much forethought, he drove closer to town and to the Sawyer Shores development, the small enclave of houses built by the company now headed by his friend Hart Sawyer. Then he pulled up to the modern Craftsman that his buddy had moved into a few months before. Striding up the walkway, pizza in hand, he realized he'd not dropped in on the other man since he'd lost Kim, his fiancée.

Shit.

But he didn't let that deter him. Because belatedly being a better friend beat rambling around the old house which would be both too empty and also too full of memories—of Sloane, her scent, her kiss—that he was eager to escape.

And then, of course, he had a pizza to share.

Which was the first word out of Hart's mouth when he opened the door to Eli's ring. "Pizza," he said, his gaze dropping to the box.

Eli's gaze didn't sway from his buddy. "You look like shit," he announced.

Hart grasped the edge of the cardboard and hauled both it and Eli over the threshold. "I feel like shit."

It took a moment for Eli to put it together. While he'd been at work all day, weekends were Hart's time off. The man looked disheveled and half-asleep, wearing cutoff sweatpants, a ragged T-shirt, and a couple of days' growth of beard.

As he was led toward the open living space, he noted the pyramid of beer cans on the table between the sofa and the big-screen TV.

"This doesn't look good," he murmured.

But Hart heard it. "I've been trying to get out of my head," he said, bleary-eyed. "All weekend long."

Eli abandoned the pizza to his friend and marched into the kitchen. "Coffee for you, pal, no more beer. And eat some of that pizza, stat." From what he could see, the man had been consuming his calories via the hops in his favorite IPA and not much else.

Once the carafe was full of a strong brew, he carried a large mug of the black stuff to his friend, who was sitting on the couch and looked to be onto his third slice. "Good," Eli said, putting the coffee into the other man's free hand. "Keep eating and drink that."

With the third piece of pizza demolished and halfway through his second mug, Hart appeared slightly more human. He glanced down at the steaming beverage. "Damn it," he said. "I'm going to be up all night."

"Half-caf," Eli said. "Maybe even quarter-caf." He'd found both kinds of grounds in the freezer and mixed the two in the filter basket.

Still, Hart set the mug aside and then eyed the pizza with a cautious eye. "I think I better slow down on that, too."

Eli dropped into an adjacent armchair. "What's this about getting out of your head?"

"I said that?" Hart grimaced. "You woke me from a beer-nap. They make a guy stupid."

Maybe so. Because Eli had been thinking, thinking hard, and staying *in* his head was quickly becoming an imperative. His head was where common sense, logic, and experience prevailed. It was elsewhere—his dick—that was too happy to recall and too willing to be sidetracked by memories of Sloane's hands on his skin, her mouth on his chest, his belly, then sucking in the throbbing, aching length of him.

Yeah, his dick was more than willing to give all the thinking over to the little head, which was eager for a repeat performance with his house guest.

Yanking his mind back to the present, he leaned forward to brace his elbows on his knees. "Do you want to talk?" Looking into his friend's face, the lines of it stark with weariness, compassion leaked into Eli's chest, stirring a familiar ache. "I've said it before—that I can understand, at least a little. Grieving…well, you know my history."

But he'd never revealed his own intense anguish to anyone until yesterday, when he'd told Sloane about his midnight excursions to the rooftop. He'd surprised the hell out of himself by telling her, but it had come out and he couldn't regret it.

"I…" Hart shrugged, then lapsed into silence.

Eli allowed that, sitting with his friend in the heavy quiet, unspoken emotion as much in the room as the two of them. It sat with you, Eli recalled now, or on you, weighing down your shoulders or pushing on your chest. Maybe it was enough, for now, for him to be here. For him not to let his friend be alone with it.

In the distance, a bong sounded. A grandfather clock, Hart's actual grandfather's clock, that had belonged to the man who'd been a namesake of the Sawyer Beach founder and who'd also established the construction company his grandson now led.

The noise roused Hart. He stirred, and took up the mug again, the liquid inside likely cooled, but he didn't seem to notice. "Talk to me about something else, Eli."

"Like what?"

"I don't know." Hart took a swallow of the

coffee. "Where are you with those dating apps? Did you finish your profiles?"

Their phone call—the night Sloane had showed up on his doorstep in the storm—seemed like a million years ago. "I think I've abandoned that direction for now."

"Does that mean you found what you were looking for when you left Thursday's poker game?"

Eli gave his friend this, too. It was good, actually, that Hart was emerging from that dark yet numbing lake of grief to express an interest outside of its murky depths.

"More than what I was looking for," he admitted. "I...did I tell you about my neighbor and her little girl?"

As Hart listened, Eli explained the circumstances of the two coming to live at his house and even sketched, in broad terms, Sloane's difficult upbringing and marriage. Then he, without being explicit, told the other man about the one-night stand with Sloane, confident he wouldn't broadcast the information.

"Okay," Hart said, sitting back in the cushions. "So why do you seem conflicted instead of satisfied?"

Eli hesitated.

"Something's bothering you. Spit it out."

He opened his mouth to reveal that their single night had merely served to sharpen his appetite. And damn, if that wasn't true. But...

"Despite everything she's experienced, she wants to believe in happy endings," Eli heard himself confess instead. "'Somebody gets to have that,' she said to me yesterday...and I...I didn't jump right up and agree."

Hart's eyebrows rose. "You don't believe it

yourself?"

"For sure I know I don't like being the one to put a cynical cast over her world view." He ran both hands through his hair. "And…yeah, I probably don't believe it for me. That happy ending business, if by happy ending we mean me and a wife and kids."

Hart didn't say anything.

"Look, I've already been through enough emotions in my lifetime to stuff a grizzly."

"Interesting way of putting it."

"Damn it." Eli shoved his hands through his hair again, feeling defensive and irritated. "I merely want my simple and straightforward bachelor life. Unencumbered. And if it's not too much to ask, uninhibited."

"Okay," Hart said, his tone reasonable. "I got it. You want a lifetime of condoms."

Eli blinked. "What?"

"Uninhibited and unencumbered. You're looking at rolling on rubbers until the end of your days. Men can father babies into their eighties, you know."

"Now I need a beer," Eli muttered.

Hart suddenly grinned, his face transforming from a carved mask into something that looked like the man he'd been before. "I think I'm having fun."

"So glad to be the source of your amusement," Eli grumbled. "And how you're looking at me is wigging me out, by the way. You and Baby Sally should start a club. You could choose a cause and scare people into supporting it."

Hart even laughed now, though it sounded somewhat rusty. "I'm going to let that Baby Sally comment slide for the moment. Let's take it to the core, Eli. If you could have anything right this minute, what would it be?"

"More Sloane," he said without thinking twice about it. "More Sloane, but in a conscious, intentional way, with no niggling worrying that passion is oversaturating the colors and without the risk of anyone—okay, her—getting swept into believing there is more to it than the...the pure bodily function that it is."

He looked off into the distance, moody now, grouchy as that grizzly he'd mentioned because with his sisters out of the house his life was supposed to be *less* complicated. *Less* stressful.

"Bodily function," Hart echoed. "*Hmm.* You've never been in love, right?"

Eli glanced over. "I suppose not, unless an excellent turf builder counts."

Hart started laughing again. "Keep fighting the good fight, buddy. I'm on your side, no matter what happens."

Nothing was going to *happen*, Eli thought, scowling on his ride back to his house. The whole point of this trial bachelor period was the absence of things *happening*. No emergency school projects, no frenemies wreaking havoc, no freak-outs about grades, boys, or making the athletic team.

It was supposed to be a taste of the relaxed, responsibility-free—well, dependents-free at least—life in his future.

Pulling into the garage, he noted Sloane's car on the street and decided he didn't feel anything in particular about the return of mother and daughter. So much so, that he'd pretend she and Paige weren't there and he'd make a comfortable place for himself on the family room couch and go potato with sports and the remains of the cold pizza.

The downstairs was quiet, like his future bachelor pad would be. He smiled to himself and made for the kitchen where he tossed down the pizza box and flipped open the top. Then he heard a child's laugh and his head turned. A mother's answering murmur changed the trajectory of his feet.

Swept up by the sounds, he headed for the stairs.

At the noise of knuckles against the doorjamb, Sloane looked away from where Paige was selecting her story time choices from the bookshelf in the play room. Eli stood, framed by the white wood trim, a working man from his tanned face to his scuffed boots. Even his forearms, bared by a flannel shirt rolled to the elbows, looked capable and powerful.

Distracting.

Averting her gaze from the male splendor of him, she tugged on the hem of the T-shirt she wore with yoga pants. "Hey," she said, her tone light and breezy. "I threw together a pasta salad. The leftovers are in the refrigerator."

"I brought home some leftovers too—pizza."

Paige glanced around, her hair still damp from her bath and dressed in pajamas decorated with pink cats. "E!" she said. "Time for books."

He smiled at the little girl. Sloane steeled her heart. Yesterday she'd come to a conclusion. Her lonely childhood and her disastrous marriage, which should have stomped the sentimentalism right out of her, had instead made her vulnerable to the atmosphere contained within this family house.

At another time, she would have been unsusceptible. But without her own roof to shelter under, she'd fallen prey to looking at the King home and at Eli himself through a gauzy, glittery veil, giving her a star-spangled view. Remember her fantasy of the man's smart and beautiful wife and the two sons they would share?

A fabrication.

*Somebody* gets to have that, she'd said aloud in the garage the day before, but whether that somebody was or was not Eli or that somebody was *anybody*…it was time for her to let go of her preoccupation with the idea. Her concern should only be about her own life and to that end, she'd rededicated herself, her thoughts, and her energies to her priority.

Blinders off! Rose-colored glasses gone! Fantasy cap tossed away!

Time to get down to the business of mothering Paige, her number one concern and the sole person who filled her heart. The little girl was enough to keep a single woman taking the next step and the next and then the one after that. Her daughter was all Sloane needed.

With a short stack of reading material in one arm, Paige stepped toward the bedroom, then halted near Eli. "What's this?" she asked him, pointing to the height markings on the jamb.

He took a step away and looked at the ink lines, names, and dates. "Ah. This is where we kept a record of how my sisters and I grew. Every year on our birthdays, we'd draw a line to show how tall we were."

"My birthday is Saturday," Paige said.

"I heard that." He shot a quick glance at Sloane.

Suddenly she remembered chattering to him about the upcoming event. They'd been naked, in bed, and she blushed recalling how she'd been sprawled over his length, blissed out on whatever endorphins were released upon orgasming.

Despite her embarrassment, the heat on her face took a little trek down the rest of her body. Ignoring an attraction that was of no use to a woman who had other, more important considerations, she cleared her throat, preparing to usher her child toward bed.

"Let's see how you measure up," Eli said, moving aside and positioning Paige with his hands on her shoulders.

Her daughter took direction seriously, holding still with her eyes and chin level. Eli put a fingertip to the wood as placeholder, then pulled Paige away. "You're much bigger than Lynnie and Molly were at four," he said in admiring tones. "See?"

Her little girl peered at the doorjamb, a small smile on her face. Then she grinned and looked to Sloane. "Big!" she told her mother.

"Yes, big." Sloane shot a cursory glance and then took a second look. The King twins were of above-average height, at least from her five-foot-three perspective, but Paige did have half an inch on them when they were the same age. "You're growing up too fast."

Truer words, she thought with a pang, as she settled her daughter into bed. Wasn't it just last week that she'd put her down in a crib?

At Paige's insistence, Eli stayed for story time. They read a book about a dog, a cat, and then *The Paper Bag Princess*, the child's latest favorite. "Bad Ronald," she declared in a sleepy voice at the end.

"Yeah," Eli said. "Beware of the Ronalds of the world, Paige." He sent Sloane a smile. "Well, as I tell my sisters, beware of *all* boys."

Words to live by, she thought, as she tucked her little girl beneath the covers and then bestowed the compulsory three kisses. One for a good night, one for a good sleep, and one for good dreams.

With a night-light left burning and Boo settled on the foot of the bed, she and Eli retreated from the room. Sloane repeated the all-important word to herself again—*beware*. Because that sentimentalism was beckoning again, making it too easy to cast herself and Eli in the role of mommy and daddy, now heading downstairs for the evening, their child securely on the way to dreamland.

"She's going to grow up, you know," Eli said. "Faster than you think."

Alarmed, Sloane's bare feet stuttered on the runner. She'd just reorganized her thinking and screwed her head on straight by putting her daughter once again at the center of her universe.

"Then she'll be out on her own," the man continued.

Where would Sloane be without her focal point? Her feet stuttered again, and this time Eli grabbed her hand, squeezing to steady her.

"Are you all right?" he asked, still retaining his grip as they began descending the steps.

"I don't know," she admitted, letting him tug her into the kitchen. "I can barely imagine her four, let alone fourteen or twenty-four."

"You can't stop time," Eli said.

Slipping her hand from his, she frowned. "I guess not." That was true. It would be just another kind of delusion to ignore the fact that every day her daughter grew older. Grew away from her.

Without asking, he poured a glass of wine and put it into her hand. Then he poured another for himself. "Cheers," he said, clinking the rims.

"Not a kissing toast this time?" The words tumbled out of her.

His hand froze halfway to his mouth. He cut his gaze to hers.

She froze too, heat flashing across her skin, receding, flashing again.

Like the lights at a railroad crossing. Yet another warning.

Heeding it, she glanced away and wiped her face free of any expression, her lips turning up in what she hoped was a pleasant, neutral curve.

But when Eli tilted back his head to take a long swallow of wine, her gaze shifted to track the movement of the muscles of his throat.

How could that be so sexy? And why was she allowing herself to be distracted just as she'd re-righted herself as a single-focus single mom?

*She's going to grow up, you know.*

Shaking off the thought, she took a sip of wine and moved toward the kitchen table. A map of the western United States was spread upon it and she saw the markings he'd penned. "Always trying to steer them right?" she asked.

He came nearer, standing close enough that if she cocked her elbow she'd touch his arm. How could so small an idea loom so large in her head? But she couldn't get her mind off that short bit of space between them, the one she should regard as an insurmountable gulf.

Eli leaned down to trace his finger over the route lined in red. "They disregarded my suggested travel plan during hour one."

She laughed. "They're growing up too."

"Definitely. Nora and Allison...I accept that with those two. It's still hard to think of the twins leaving home, though."

"Did I hear right?" With exaggerated wide eyes, she turned her head to look at him. "Are you saying you'll miss them?"

He cast her a sidelong glance. "I detect a note of feigned disbelief."

"Well, you have seemed impossibly composed about the whole idea of them flying free of the nest...outside of your compulsive need to micromanage this trip, that is."

Turning, he set aside his glass. "Sloane Clarke, I believe you think you see right through me."

At the teasing note she turned too, the both of them now face-to-face. "You're not so hard to read."

His eyebrows rose. "Oh, yeah? What am I thinking at this moment?"

The truth was, the challenging light in his eyes made him harder to decipher. So she put her wineglass aside as well, then crossed her arms over her chest and slowly rolled her gaze down his broad chest to his lean hips and long legs. On the return trip, she went even slower, because...

Because she was sidetracked again, remembering all those muscles and that length of him naked. A new warmth suffused her skin and she had to curl her fingers into fists so as not to reach out and touch him. But if she indulged...

It would be the soft flannel of his shirt first, just

the barest skim of it with her fingertips, and then she'd find the small buttons, unfastening them one by one until she could reach the hot flesh over hard muscle underneath. Her breathing became shallow and she felt the hair at the edges of her scalp prickle.

It was impossible not to touch him, so she did. As she'd imagined, the very tips of her fingers ghosting over the flannel, starting at his shoulders and then moving in the direction of the untucked tails.

"Hold still," she said. "Please don't move." Her head was in the game...this game, the touch and tease game, and she refused to think beyond this moment, this man. Now.

"Do you know what you're doing?" he asked, his voice rough, even as she also heard what went unsaid. The man didn't ask her to stop nor did he move away.

Her gaze followed her fingers. "You mean do I know what this *isn't* about?"

"Yes." He could speak through gritted teeth.

Smiling a little at that, she progressed to step two, finding the topmost fastened button. Her heart thrummed in her throat and her breasts swelled, aching, just like that place between her legs.

"This means I have needs," she said. "I thought...but I'm not..." All day she'd been telling herself that looking clear-eyed at the world meant embracing her single motherhood. And she did. She loved being Paige's mom and was fine with raising her daughter alone. But...

The complete reality was that she wasn't only that one thing. Yes, she was a mother. But she was also a woman, living, breathing, *wanting*. That part of herself had been laid aside during the previous four years.

"You're just so pretty," she said, moving on to another fastening and then another. "Nobody could blame me."

"I might." Eli scowled. "What's this about prettiness? I've heard that before and I didn't like it then."

She smiled up at him, still unbuttoning. "You remember I've seen you with barrettes in your hair."

His hands found her shoulders, dug in. "Sloane, I'm serious." His gaze bore into hers. "This isn't about romance," he warned.

"I'm not asking for romance," she replied. "I'm merely asking for *this*." And she spread the two sides of his now-opened shirt, baring him.

He sucked in a sharp breath, his chest expanding, his belly hollowing. She felt another rush of heat, and her body softened inside, her womb growing heavy. With her nails, she drew a path over his nipples toward his waistband. "And *this*," she said.

But before she could lay claim to another inch of him, he pounced.

His bigger body propelled her three feet in an instant, her back thumping against the flat surface of the refrigerator. Her gasping mouth was then filled with his tongue, his lips hot and urgent on hers, and she sagged, grabbing hold of his sides to keep from sliding to his feet. He grunted, pushing his hips against hers, and feeling the bulge there, her blood ignited. Reaching for his hair, she tangled her fingers in the long strands as his big hands slid to the back of her thighs and hefted her up. She parted her legs to wrap her ankles at the small of his back and they both groaned as he shoved against her, his heavy, denim-covered sex fusing with her heat.

His lips raced from hers to her cheek, her jaw, and then he was kissing her neck, open-mouthed and almost desperate as she let her head drop to give him more access. She drove her hips upward, wanting more sensation, wanting everything male about him against her female parts because this act was about primal need and primitive differences.

Base desire.

He could be any male body, she told herself as they dove into another wet and almost violent kiss. He thrust against her, and she tipped her hips yet again to take more, to ask for more.

"I want everything," she said against his mouth. "Give me all you have."

In another place and time she might be amazed at her passion and lack of self-consciousness, but Eli's spring break had liberated her as well, it seemed. With another groan, he let go of her legs, controlling her slide to the floor. When she was steady on her feet, he whipped her shirt over her head.

"Oh, shit," he said, his face flushed, his gaze trained on her breasts. "You mean to kill me." No bra tonight, and they felt full and hyper-sensitive, the tips beaded. His head lowered and he took a nipple into his mouth, suction and heat sending shafts of pleasure rocketing through her body.

He sucked with aggressive pleasure, and then she was holding his head to her, thinking she might come from just this, from just this man's mouth. He switched to her other breast, taking as much as he could into his mouth and slid his hands into the back of her yoga pants, clutching at her like he was afraid she might make a break for it.

Which was so far from the truth and he must

know it, because her nails dug into his scalp and she was chanting, pleading, praising. "Good, good, good," between wordless moans of approval.

His head lifted and his breathing was ragged, his chest rising and falling as if he was sprinting. He stared at her, his face—God, so pretty, no matter how he hated that—communicating the same hunger driving her on. "My room—"

But she was already shaking her head because that was too far and her excitement too demanding, because what they were doing was all about now, now, *now*. Life and liberation were much too fleeting, she knew that.

"Sloane…"

She began shoving down her pants, taking her panties with them. Her movements jerky, she stepped free of the fabric, her heart racing. Then she attacked the button of his jeans, the material fighting her until he put his hands over hers and moved them off. "I've got this, love," he said, a little smile softening the harsh lines of his face.

*Love.*

Her heart tripped.

Stupid, stupid, she told herself. Stupid that a casual endearment could weaken her knees and hitch her breathing.

*Love.*

To ignore the echo of it, she took hold of his shirt even as he continued to work at his jeans and then his boots. The flannel tangled at his wrists and she might have laughed at the awkward undressing but there was nothing funny in the way she was feeling, that it was necessary, so vital, for them to connect once again.

Right this instant.

Now.

He tossed a foil packet and then his wallet onto a nearby countertop. She heard her breathing, rapid and raspy, as he turned to her. "Come here," he said, hauling her close for another consuming kiss. She molded herself to his naked skin, her arms around his neck and one leg twining his calf.

*Good*, she thought, and *more*.

He boosted her onto the cool tile surface, her hot, bare skin barely registering the contrast in temperature as she drew him between her open legs. His palms cupped her face, turning it upward for another bold kiss.

Her tongue tangled with his and she reached down to caress his stiff shaft, reveling in the heavy jut of it, and was bold herself as she stroked him, her hand claiming the long, hard inches. He crowded closer and the back of her knuckles bumped his belly as she continued to roughly stroke him.

He broke the kiss on a gasp. "God, Sloane." Breathing hard, he pressed his forehead against hers and stilled her hand. "Too much."

"Bad?"

"No." A laugh choked out. "But the way I want you…"

She tilted her chin to catch his mouth again. Before the kiss could catch fire he lifted his head and pulled her hand from him. "Condom," he muttered and she reached for it blindly, her hand finding foil then passing it over.

He was prepared, they were protected, but he hesitated now, and she made a greedy sound in the back of her throat. "Eli. Please."

"I like you eager," he whispered, and one of his

hands ventured between her legs, where she was open and wet and ready for him.

"I am eager," she agreed, arching into his delicate touch. One long finger filled her. "I'm eager *now*."

Nuzzling the side of her head, he chuckled and her hips moved in silent entreaty, wanting more than this taunting penetration. His thumb circled her clit and she jerked, her body pulling in that lone, teasing finger. "Please."

Eli groaned as her muscles squeezed. "Were you sore after…"

"I don't care," she said, digging her nails into his shoulders. "I want it. I want to be sore. I want to feel you tomorrow."

He groaned again.

"Come inside me."

His hand withdrew to be replaced with the blunt head, pushing to part her soft, wet tissue. He was big, no doubt, and she breathed in and deliberately relaxed to allow him entry. He pressed his face to her neck as he worked his way inside by slow degrees and she felt consumed by him and by lust and by sensation. *Good.*

Pleasure rolled over her skin, curling her toes and tightening her nipples to even more painful points. The edge of his thumb found one and she cried out, her body opening to him for full, flagrant penetration.

Groin to groin, they both stilled, breathing hard. Then he was moving, driving, diving into her heat without restraint. Her head fell back and she thought that pleasure was too tame a word, too long a word, because this feeling was sharp and strong and deep. It built in layers, steps, and she climbed them, all the while urging Eli on with her fingers digging into his shoulders.

He whispered to her, now it was his praise in her ears. *You feel so right, yes, like that, you are so slick, so hot.* And finally, *oh, God, unbelievable.*

On that, his thumb found her clit again, providing sweet, welcome friction, and he was pumping heavily, thrust after thrust, his breath harsh in her ears and she took that last step, climbed to orgasm, and flung herself over. Dimly aware, she heard his low groan and felt his final lunge, then he stilled, well-planted, their connection unbroken.

Endless.

Until he moved. His head lifted and he took her face between his palms, his expression still lust-drunk yet sated at the same time. She could look no better, as she felt blissfully ruined. She swallowed and then her gaze dropped, snagging on raw scratches marring the skin covering his broad shoulders.

"I did that," she said, aghast, and then, more aghast, felt tears begin to leak from the outside corners of her eyes. Her gaze lifted, and she looked at him through a watery haze. "I'm sorry."

"Love," he said again, and kissed away her tears. "They're nothing." A gentle kiss was pressed to her mouth. "I don't mind feeling you."

*I want to feel you tomorrow.*

She'd said that, dangerous words, because this act was supposed to be one for the immediate moment only. They were about now and now alone.

"Don't look so stricken," he said, and kissed her again. His head lifted and the tender expression on his face made her scoot away in alarm. He took the hint and pulled back, moving to dispose of the condom.

Sloane used the opportunity to slip off the countertop and land on her feet, ignoring the wobble of her knees. As she glanced around for her clothes, feeling clumsy and vulnerable and impatient to be covered, Eli gathered her close, subduing her immediate protest by closing his arms around her.

"Shh," he said. "Let me hold you." His embrace was easy, practiced, steady, not the least bit panicked like her frightened and rollicking heart.

He encouraged her to lean against him and the act was so novel that she allowed it, letting him support her as she strove to find some calm. But it was certainty she discovered instead. A knowledge that dropped upon her like a shroud or perhaps an anvil, something weighty and dire.

She'd fallen in love, she thought, on another sudden jolt of fear.

That had to be what caused this queasy, unbalanced, and yet undeniably giddy sensation.

She'd fallen in love with Eli.

With his every tender look and passionate touch. With his easy grins and his ingrained sense of responsibility. Squeezing shut her eyes, she called herself every kind of fool.

And yet she didn't move.

"Now that's better," he said, pressing a kiss to her hair.

*Now.*

And forever.

# Chapter 11

Eli awoke alone in bed and stared at the ceiling, awaiting a regret that didn't come. The empty pillow next to his told him that Sloane had once again escaped sometime in the night. The fact she didn't linger beside him into the morning told him she wasn't nurturing expectations or making assumptions.

What they'd shared last night hadn't been a mistake then, he thought, relieved.

Still, throwing back the covers, he decided to proceed with caution. He'd tread carefully, take her pulse, and try to walk back the situation if it seemed necessary.

That they'd spent two nights together didn't have to mean he'd sent the wrong message, and he very much hoped he had not, but for four years she'd gone without sex…and been without someone in her corner.

He hated that for her.

Climbing into the shower and then getting ready for work, he reminded himself that he wasn't the man to commit to the kind of relationship a mother and child deserved long-term.

In that regard he'd given and given and given and now was his time to break free of those fetters.

Pushing open his bedroom door, he smelled coffee in the air. Resolved to making sure all was understood between him and Sloane, he headed for the kitchen, then heard Paige calling his name.

He looked up to see the little girl and Boo on the staircase landing. She beckoned him. "This way! A party!"

Stronger men than he had been unable to resist a cute kid and a shaggy dog. So he mounted the steps then allowed himself to be led into the playroom. Tea party-sized cups and plates sat on the small plastic table. Baby Sally perched on a stack of books on the seat of a molded green plastic chair. She wore what appeared to be a mummy gown made of toilet paper and familiar barrettes in a messy updo.

Paige gestured to a place across from the doll. "You there."

He moved aside the chair and sat cross-legged on the floor. Boo joined him with a rattle of his collar and a doggy groan.

The little girl chose the yellow chair. "This is not my birthday party."

"Right."

"That's Saturday. Are you coming?"

"I wouldn't miss it."

She eyed him with doubt as she picked up a small plastic teapot.

"I promise." When she continued to look at him, he added, "I have a present."

That seemed to mollify her. *Mental note: buy a present.*

She pretended to pour into the little cups. "This is a breakfast party."

"It's very nice." He waited until all were "full" before he picked up his own.

Paige mimicked him. "Mommy says you have four little girls."

Looking around the playroom, he could see why she'd think his sisters were still small. Beyond the books and dolls and blocks and tea sets, there was also a stack of board games taller than Paige, including Chutes & Ladders and Candyland, which he could have sworn he burned years ago, following the torturous monotony of yet another evening playing them.

Like the garage, everything in the space was going to have to go too, he realized. No one would want the house with all these shabby childhood artifacts left behind.

All these memories.

He shook himself. "The little girls you're talking about are almost grown up. And remember, you know two of them—they've watched you when your mom was out. Lynnie and Molly."

"Oh," Paige said, and set down her cup to fuss with Baby Sally who was staring at Eli like she hungered for a man-sized snack with her tea. "But you don't want any more little girls."

He averted his gaze from the doll, then took a moment to wonder if Paige's comment meant she'd asked Sloane about that, about him wanting kids. A little girl. *Shit.*

Casting his gaze back to the child, he watched her move the doll's cup closer to her plastic hand. Being in this room reminded him of the bustle and chaos of a four-girl household, their screeches and shrieks, the fights over clothes, the drama over stolen diaries.

The triumphant grins as they shared good news and stellar report cards.

The tears he'd blotted over bad news and lousy grades.

Exhausting.

But that didn't stop a traitorous fondness warming his heart as he looked upon the towhead, with her pillow-mussed hair and button nose. *You don't want any more little girls.*

He didn't, he reminded himself, but still his mouth opened. "Paige—"

A voice from downstairs interrupted whatever unwary admission he might have made. Sloane called up the stairs. "Breakfast!"

Man, dog, and child rattled down the steps together.

In the kitchen, Sloane gave him a quick scan, her expression betraying nothing. "Sausage and French toast?"

He crossed to the coffee maker. "You don't owe me—"

"I know," she said, sounding testy. "But I made enough for three."

"Well, sure, great then." Feeling like an ass, he slipped his phone from his pocket and checked the screen, as if it might provide unprompted hints about how to handle an awkward morning-after when apparently the awkward-feeling partner in this situation was him. *Shit.*

Setting his cell on the counter, with his other hand he opened the cabinet for a mug. His sidelong look at Sloane didn't give away her state of mind. Perhaps she should sit in for him at the next poker night, because whether she held four aces or a fistful of junk, no one would guess.

He topped off his mug and then, annoyed with himself, paused beside her on his way to the table. Despite how collected she appeared, he couldn't help asking, "Are you okay?"

Just after midnight he'd swum out of sleep to find her kissing a path from his chest to his rising cock. For an instant he'd thought it a sweet dream, but the warmth and wet of her mouth had been real, as well as her whispering she'd always wanted to wake a man in just that way. He'd had his own similar fantasies, and he'd managed to rearrange her soft skin and heated limbs until they could both be pleasured by each other's mouth at the same time.

"I'm fine," she said now, and moved quickly away, quick enough that it stirred the air and when he breathed in, her scent came too, bringing him back to his bed, her body, her sighs and moans.

He sure as hell didn't regret any of that.

At the table, he applied himself to the food, and paused without thinking when Paige asked him to pour syrup and cut her piece of toast. Looking up from that task, he caught Sloane standing by the sink and staring at him with wide eyes that communicated…what? Alarm?

"Love," he called to her with soft concern, beginning to rise.

"No." She flapped her hand and turned away.

"Sloane—" The chime of an incoming call interrupted and his hand went to his pocket. No phone. He glanced around.

"Here," Sloane said, scooping the device from the counter where he'd left it by the coffee, and walking it over. Her face was blank when she said, "Alanna is calling."

The ring died before he had a chance to accept or decline the call. Seconds later, the voicemail icon appeared on the screen. He stared at it.

"One of your dates?" Sloane asked, her tone pleasant.

"Tonight," he replied, terse.

She seemed perfectly at ease with the idea. "That should be fun."

Then why did it feel like a mistake, he asked himself, and asked himself that same question again hours later when he walked into the new Sawyer Beach food hall located in what had once been the town drugstore. The sizeable building dated back to the early 1900s and they'd saved the original soda fountain, complete with counter and stools, which was now run by a local creamery. Sectioned off into separate spaces, six other eateries prepared and sold food ranging from artisan pizza to sushi to deli. A center bar offered spirits and local brew and there was also a coffee cart in one corner. Tables were plentiful, four-tops and six-tops and long ones flanked by benches that would seat dozens.

The hall had been opened for about a month and obviously still drew a curious crowd. Though a weeknight, it was jam-packed, the noise nearly deafening. Eli didn't know how he'd pick out his date from the quick glimpse of a photo on Sophie

Daggett's phone. He scanned the crowd and his eye caught on an attractive woman who was waving an arm.

Her free hand held that of a boy who appeared to be six or seven.

So he looked onward.

But he couldn't miss that the woman who'd been waving was on the move. She came forward, towing the child until she stopped in front of Eli, a friendly smile on her face. "Alanna?" he ventured to guess.

"Yes. You're Eli?"

At his nod, they exchanged friendly handshakes. Then she drew the boy forward. "This is Brandon. His dad and I share custody, but we had our wires crossed. I discovered at the last minute you and I will have a chaperone for the evening."

"Ah." Holding out his hand again, Eli greeted the boy. "Nice to meet you."

He wanted to turn right around and go home. Not because of pretty Alanna. Not because of the kid. And not because of the food hall either, though the sound of echoing voices was drilling into his brain like an auger bit. The truth was, it had been a long day at work preceded by a night of less than stellar sleep. Sure, there'd been stellar other things during the dark hours, but not shut-eye.

He was running low on geniality, even for a pleasant stranger and her little boy.

So maybe sleeping with Sloane had been a mistake after all.

But dwelling on that wouldn't improve the current situation, so he placed a casual arm around Alanna and a hand on the boy's shoulder to usher them toward the drinks station. "What can I get you,

Alanna? A glass of wine? Brandon, would you like a soda? Juice?"

They probably answered, but their voices and all the other sounds faded away as he caught sight of Sloane standing in line at the pizza station, wearing a formfitting dress and a pair of beige high heels. At her side, Paige hopped from foot to foot, a pink bow in her hair matching the pink sneakers on her feet. At her mother's other elbow hovered a man.

A man Eli's age, or thereabouts. His suit looked well-tailored, well-pressed, and he wore his black hair close-cropped. As Eli watched, the guy leaned close to whisper something in Sloane's ear. Laughing, she put her hand on his arm.

A searing heat burned in Eli's gut and began to crawl through his bloodstream. A sudden sickness, he tried telling himself. A belated reaction to the lunch he'd consumed hours ago, a quesadilla and an iced tea one of the front office staff had brought back from their favorite taco truck.

He'd come to the food hall straight from the office, freshening up in the locker room and changing into clean clothes before leaving the nursery. At breakfast, he'd not taken the opportunity to ask Sloane about her plans for the day.

They were none of his business, of course.

But it meant he had no clue about the identity of her companion.

And the truth was, he'd not considered she might be looking for something—someone—who offered more than Eli...who had made sure he offered her nothing but string-less fun or whatever the fuck he'd termed it.

So why was he taken aback that she was making

nice with a man who wore a suit, a tie, and polished dress shoes that Eli would scuff the first time he looked at them? So why was he on his heels that she was dating someone while living in his house? That she was with some other guy when she'd so recently been in his bed?

Because, after all, he was doing the very same thing.

A tug on his shirtsleeve had him blinking. He glanced down, saw the boy with the inquiring look on his face and drew a complete blank. "Uh…Blake?"

"Brandon," his mother said. Alanna. Alanna of the dark wavy hair and the warm brown eyes. She and her son didn't deserve to have dinner with an uncaring asshole any more than Sloane and Paige had deserved to have breakfast with one.

"Yes. Right," he said, and worked on a smile. Raising his voice to be heard over the din, he asked what they were thinking to have for their meal.

Pizza, of course.

He didn't let his dismay show on his face. He didn't let his gaze shoot toward his housemates now waiting for their own order of wood-fired dough, sauce, and cheese baked in the brick oven shipped straight from Sicily.

On a deep breath, he focused on his current companions. "Have you been to the food hall before? This is my first time."

Conversation began easily enough. The piercing din lessened to a reasonable level and he learned that Alanna was in real estate and Brandon the second grade. The boy had a cat and a hamster. Eli shared his sisters once had a rabbit that they sneaked into their beds at night.

Still, it all felt like a mistake.

Like he was in the wrong place at the wrong time.

Or maybe just with the wrong people.

Sloane's coworker Will Mooney shuffled forward in the line to order pizza and she followed, one hand on the back of Paige's head to steer her in the same direction. The child took a skip and a jump, her attention preoccupied with the art project she'd brought home from daycare—a little figure made of a cork and a glued-on scrap of gingham fabric as clothes, along with silly googly eyes.

"We should have ordered ahead from the office," Will said, his grimace doing nothing to mar his model-quality good looks.

"Mmm," she said, barely listening.

He glanced down. "A few minutes' wait isn't that bad, is it?" he asked, jostling her arm with a friendly elbow. "You look like somebody stole your precious pencil sharpener."

It was an office joke that Sloane needed her sharpened pencils to function and that only the electric device she kept secure on a corner of her desk could provide the perfect points. "I'm good, fine."

Will turned and looked at her more closely. "Earth to Sloane."

She blinked, shook herself a little, and met his eyes. "I'm sorry. What?"

"You *did* think the meeting went well, didn't you?" The dark brown skin of Will's forehead wrinkled in concern.

"I did, really." The two of them had consulted

with a prospective client that afternoon, a task usually taken on by Alice and Joe, their accounting firm's owners. But the head pair had allocated the job to she and Will this time, expressing confidence in their abilities to represent them well. "I was just lost in my own thoughts for a minute."

Because she'd caught sight of Eli and his date at the very instant of their meeting, or so she'd surmised, watching him shake hands with the attractive woman and then with the little boy at her side.

Stupid, that the presence of the child had shaken her so. Over the course of the day, she'd become convinced she'd been wrong to believe herself in love with Eli. First off, she barely knew the man. Secondly, what experience did she have with love anyway?

From the beginning she'd been aware of her little crush on him and it seemed a couple—okay, more— orgasms had given her infatuation some added bells, whistles, and sparkling fairy dust. That's all. Still, seeing him with another single mom and her son, when he'd been so adamant that was the antithesis of his bachelor break requirements…stung.

They reached the counter and she gave Will the go-ahead. He had a wife and child himself, and was eager to get home to them. After he placed his order, it was her turn, and then they moved aside to make way for the people behind them. Noting that Eli had joined the long line, Sloane purposefully chose to wait at a distance from the pick-up counter and for added insurance, turned her back so she wouldn't be forced to acknowledge her housemate.

Fortunately, Will didn't seem to notice or at least didn't comment upon her maneuvering. He stayed close, engaging with Paige about her cork doll. *Such a nice guy.*

Eli was a nice guy too, and she wasn't any more truly enamored with him that she was with her work colleague. Right?

Okay, there were the luscious kisses and the light-bending orgasms on Eli's side, but that was just sex. Just. Sex.

Everybody knew not to conflate sexual fulfillment with an emotional attachment.

And if she hadn't known before, she'd certainly learned after her disastrous marriage not to attach herself to a man for hollow reasons.

"Did I tell you I talked to Alice?" Will asked now.

Sloane rounded on him. "*What?*"

"She phoned this morning. She said she unexpectedly had a couple of reception bars so checked in."

Why had their boss called Will? But he did have the more senior position in the firm and Alice had no way of knowing Sloane's residential issues, as she hadn't shared them with Will. But now she could rectify that. "I should call her myself," she said, her spirits lifting as she began to dig into her purse for her phone.

"Don't bother. She expected to be out of range again at their desert campground and I lost her while we were talking. But they're having a great vacation and will be back in the next couple of days or so…definitely in time for Paige's party, she told me."

"Right," Sloane said, her mood lowering a notch. "I can speak with her then." Still, she saw the light at the end of the tunnel. Soon she'd be back on her own, and away from Eli King and whatever minor sway he held over her.

Then she heard her name called and Sloane laughed when Paige performed another little hop-skip. With a hot-from-the-oven pizza waiting, the world couldn't help but appear brighter.

Will took his selection and left for home, while Paige insisted on staying to eat theirs at one of the food hall tables. She couldn't blame the child for wanting to soak up the lively atmosphere, but she found them a corner table and sat across from her daughter with her back to the room—acting as a screen between Paige and the rest of the space. No need to risk a chance encounter with her housemate and his companions. For all she knew, Eli and his date and her child had ordered their food to go, but she didn't want Paige catching sight of Eli and doing something…foolish.

Sloane didn't trust her feckless heart, either.

Between bites of food and sips from their drinks, Sloane listened to her daughter chatter about her upcoming birthday party. At almost four, this was the first year Paige really understood that the celebrating would all be for her. They'd planned on rolled tacos and bean burritos from their favorite Mexican place, a cooler of water and juices, a piñata and a couple of other games, then cupcakes to conclude the festivities. She'd thought to make them herself, but on a whim that day had called the fancy bakery that made Paige's eyes sparkle on every visit. They promised to wow the little girl on her big day.

Even Sloane couldn't help a little wiggle of anticipation.

Once their slices were consumed, Sloane tossed the remains of the meal into a nearby garbage can and then helped her daughter from her booster seat.

Her feet hit the floor and Paige leaned left to peer around her mother. "There," she said, pointing her little finger.

There...what? Had she spotted Eli? And had he spotted them?

"It's not polite to point," Sloane said automatically. She glanced around without turning her head, seeking a discreet exit. "What do you see?" *Who?*

"The aunt," Paige said. "The aunt with chocolate."

"Oh." Sloane glanced back, confirming the sighting. Rona Dunlap stood near the center of the food hall. Dressed in a black skirted business suit and holding a pen and notebook in hand, she appeared to be scanning the crowd.

As if Sloane called her name, the older woman's gaze found her. Rona gave a start of surprise, then waved and strode over in a pair of elegant black heels, the sound of them clicking against the textured concrete floor lost in the noise of the crowd.

But Sloane and Paige's corner offered some quiet and she waited for the woman to get within range before offering a greeting and a polite smile. "Hello. You're in town again."

Rona agreed with a brisk nod and then another for Paige. "The owners of the food hall are clients. Business is brisk tonight. Did you enjoy your visit?"

"We did, it's our first visit. Paige and I liked the pizza and I guess the noisiness proves its popularity."

Rona nodded again. "Everything still on for the party Saturday?" Now she aimed a smile at Paige.

"It is." Sloane slung her purse over her shoulder,

aware her daughter's bedtime was fast approaching. "You'll make it?"

"I plan to, and Dave," she said, naming her husband.

"Good." Sloane glanced at Paige. "We need to get to a bath and bed—"

"Sloane." Rona put up a hand. "Mom will be in town tomorrow morning."

"I know. We're already scheduled to meet at the park." They'd exchanged texts and she'd prepped Paige with photos of her grandparents and a reminder of how much they were looking forward to being in the little girl's company.

"She hasn't changed her mind," Rona said quietly.

Pizza turned to lead in Sloane's stomach. She glanced down at her daughter again, whose attention was focused once more on her cork doll as she danced it through the air. "Not here. Not now."

"You need to be aware of it," Rona insisted.

"Okay," she said, as a new uneasiness crept over her. The recent cordial communications she'd exchanged with Diane had led Sloane into thinking the older woman had abandoned her idea of guardianship or had never been serious about it at all. Sloane shoved back her hair. "It's just…I'm not really prepared—"

"That's what she's counting on," Rona said. "And she knows you're alone and have no one in your corner. She'll take advantage of your vulnerability."

*You're alone and have no one in your corner.* A searing heat and pressure built behind Sloane's eyes.

"Ow, Mommy," Paige complained. "Don't hold my hand so hard."

"Sorry, baby," she said, easing her grip, then addressed the older woman. "Rona, thank you again for warning me." But the anxiety now overwhelming her barely allowed in a breath, let alone a strategy for how to cope with the threat. "I—"

"Hey," a man's voice interrupted. A man's hand landed on her back. Eli.

Sloane half-turned to him. "Um…"

Before she could think what to say or do, Paige leaped into his arms. "Look, E. Look, I made a dolly. What should I name her?"

He managed the burden of a near four-year-old easily, boosting her onto his hip and giving serious consideration to the question. "Corky?"

Page mouthed the word, looking from him then back at the little creature. "I like it."

"Good." Eli's free hand slid to Sloane's shoulder and he nudged her closer to his body. "You okay?" he asked.

"I'm, uh, fine. We were just on our way out and ran into—"

"I know Rona," he said easily, then smiled at the other woman. "How are you?"

At her affirmative reply, he glanced down at Sloane. "She's done some work on a couple of promotional campaigns for King's Nursery."

"She's Paige's aunt."

"Ah." He nodded.

"But we were just on our way." Sloane looked to her daughter. "Weren't we, baby?"

"I'm leaving too," Eli said, his arm still slung across Sloane's shoulders. "We can walk out together."

Sloane's quick survey of the area revealed no

date and no child. *Hmm.* "Okay," she agreed. "Rona, nice to see you again. We're looking forward to having you at the Saturday party."

"Yes. I'll be there." The older woman wore a speculative expression as she looked between Sloane and Eli. "This will make a difference, Sloane," she said in an approving tone. "Mom and Dad knew Eli's parents, and they know Eli. This could make a real difference."

Sloane stilled. *Oh, no.* From that expression and those words, it was obvious Rona had made a very wrong assumption. "Um…"

But the trill of a cell phone shifted the other woman's attention, and she pulled the device from her skirt pocket and put it to her ear. Sketching a wave, she walked off, obviously looking for even quieter pastures.

So before Sloane had a chance to explain to Paige's aunt or to Eli, he was steering them out the exit. They separated to climb into separate cars, and she drove away, wondering how to address Rona's cryptic comments.

Maybe Eli hadn't noticed, though that seemed unlikely. So maybe she could put Paige in a bath and then into bed, avoiding the man she herself had been in bed with the night before. Upon bestowing the ritual three good night kisses to her daughter, she could slip into her own room and seek the oblivion of sleep, avoiding all sticky questions.

Because surely Eli wanted to know what Rona had been implying.

And then there was that problem plaguing her. If Sloane wasn't in love with the man, then what feelings did she hold for him, because *something* was there. It had been in that warm rush when he'd come upon them at the food hall, and in the way her tight chest had immediately eased at his touch, in the comfort granted when he'd simply asked, *You okay?*

Yes, taking to her pillow instead of providing or seeking answers to those uncomfortable inquiries sounded like a very wise plan indeed.

So she followed through, changing out of her work clothes, helping Paige in the bath and then into pajamas, finally settling her daughter under the covers and watching her drift toward sleep. Then, widening Paige's bedroom door to step into the hall, Sloane came face-to-chest with a living, breathing obstacle to the completion of her scheme.

Because Eli effectively shut down her notion of escape with three simple words. "What's going on?" he asked.

Sloane stared up at him, the hall light finding gold threads in his brown hair and highlighting his cheekbones and the straight blade of his nose. His chin tilted downward and she looked into his eyes and their brown had a golden light in them too.

She ordered her feet to move away, to move her to a safe distance, but from here she could feel his warmth and breathe in his scent...breathe in Eli, and it buoyed her heart and made her skin flush. Her hand itched to reach out for his. To hold on.

"Love?" he prompted.

Love. There was no doubting it now or wishing it away. She could have known him for five minutes or five years and it would be the same. Of course there was no reasoning with it or understanding where it came from or why it dropped upon a person without warning. No one had figured that out with any certainty.

So, yes, Sloane could absolutely say she was in love with him, but she'd never be able to explain how she knew, not when her experience of someone caring for her was so limited. And didn't that truth make her ache?

"Sloane." His voice lowered. "You're going to have to answer me. What's going on?"

Drawing in a long breath, she accepted she couldn't ignore him completely. But though she might not have a lot, she did have her dignity. So whatever she revealed…well, it couldn't be the whole truth. Nothing could prompt her to divulge the true state of her heart.

# Chapter 12

Eli followed Sloane down the stairs to the kitchen and watched her set the kettle on the stove to boil. "Tea?" she asked him.

He folded his arms over his chest. "Answers."

With a grimace, she crossed to grab a mug and a tea bag. Then she focused on the kettle, which, of course, extended the time it took before whistling.

The silence got to her, he could tell, because she sent him a sidelong look then commented in a casual tone, "Your date ended early."

"Her boy—"

"That was her son, then?"

"Yeah. I didn't know until I met them that she had a child." And he'd made the claim, going into his bachelor spring break, that single moms were far outside his range of interest. Shit, he thought with disgust. Could he have sounded more dickish?

Eli cleared his throat. "He...Brandon...the evening didn't end because of him, though. Well, it *was* because of her son, but..."

The kettle's shriek saved him from further explanation. Or so he thought.

Once she'd made her cup of tea, she leaned against the counter and looked at Eli over the rim. "You were saying?"

Wait. Wasn't *she* supposed to be saying? He frowned at her, but then got distracted by thinking of how Sloane had looked in the food hall, in that that dress and heels. Professional. Almost untouchable. A contrast to the jeans and T-shirt girl in front of him now, the one who had let him fuck her, right in this kitchen, right on that very countertop.

Shit, that took his mind on yet another side path. How could he ever sell this place, he wondered for a moment, when the cabinets had been witness to something so raw and passionate? Maybe he should burn them first.

"Eli?"

He blinked, backtracking through his thought processes. "Okay. They went home because the boy had neglected to mention a school project due tomorrow. He has to show and tell about something he collected."

Sloane frowned. "What if he doesn't have a collection?"

"Welcome to parenthood of school-age children," Eli said, trying to break it to her gently. "Though it doesn't have to be too complicated. Plastic dinosaurs would do. A friend of Lynnie's once shared a box full of broken shoelaces."

Looking perplexed, Sloane opened her mouth.

"I never asked why," Eli said, then smiled. "Though it makes me think I could have loaned Brandon those used soccer shoes."

Sloane narrowed her eyes. "You suggested something else then."

He blew on his nails then polished them on his shirt. "Well, yeah. And I'm a little proud of it."

Her lips twitched. "Okay, I'll bite."

"Dirt."

"Dirt?"

"Dirt. Collected from various places in the vicinity of their condo—from an outside planter, from the pot of an indoor plant, from the playground on the corner. Like that."

"Dirt," she repeated again, as if still trying to puzzle it out.

"Quick to gather, simple to store…you only need some zippered sandwich bags."

"Wow," Sloane said, and he thought he detected admiration in her gaze.

"Believe me, it will be a hit, especially if he manages to capture a bug or two as well." He smiled.

She smiled back. Yeah, admiring.

"I've learned so much," she said.

"Stick with me, kid," he replied, and instantly regretted it. "I mean—"

"I know what you mean…or don't mean." She sipped from her tea, then set it aside. "I think I'll call it a night."

At her first step, he blocked her path. "Not so fast. Not before you fill me in on the situation with Rona."

She looked him straight in the eye. "You don't want to know."

He hesitated. Right. But... "She mentioned my name. My parents."

On a sigh, Sloane looked down at her bare feet, the picture of reluctance. Then she glanced up at him. "Really?"

"Really."

Another sigh. "Rona thinks her parents—Paige's grandparents, that is, who arrive tomorrow to visit Sawyer Beach for a couple of weeks—are interested in getting custody of her."

"Custody of Paige?" He stared. "What? How?"

"They've moved to Florida and love their granddaughter. They...want her."

"She's *your* daughter."

Sloane nodded. "And the daughter of their deceased son."

"But..." He shook his head, appalled. He knew the Dunlaps slightly, as they'd contracted through the nursery to redo their landscaping a few years back. It had been Allison's idea—borne out of a class project when she was a sophomore in high school—to offer a design-and-plant service through King's and he hoped some day she might expand and run that arm if it suited her. "Why do they think they can take her from you?"

Sloane shrugged. "They have the money to pursue it."

That didn't mean that they *should*, for God's sake. "Sloane—"

"It could all be talk. And it's certainly nothing for you to worry about."

"No, but..." He replayed Rona's speculative glance, then her words. "What did Rona mean about something making a real difference?"

Sloane waved her hand in a dismissive gesture, but Eli caught it midair, and held tight. "Talk to me."

On another sigh, she extricated herself from his hold and crossed her arms over her chest, tucking her hands beneath them. "I'm guessing she made the assumption that we're...connected. That your perceived presence in my life will cause Diane and Jeffrey to think twice about their plans."

Eli considered it. Vulnerable single mom, probably with very few extra pennies to engage in a legal battle, compared to a single mom backed up by a local small business owner with a stellar reputation in the community. Much harder to take on. "Meaning Rona supposes we are..."

"Boyfriend and girlfriend." Sloane made a face. "Or whatever the adult equivalent of that is."

Eli didn't think twice. "Then we are."

"Are what?"

"Boyfriend and girlfriend or the adult equivalent. No problem."

Wide-eyed, she shook her head. "Eli—"

"You just said they're here to visit for a couple of weeks. Surely we can play up a relationship well enough to discourage them from taking advantage of you."

"Eli—"

"It's for a short time. It doesn't have to mean we have actual involvement in each other's lives."

A sound argument. Anyone could see that.

Except Sloane didn't. She was already shaking her head.

More reasoning didn't get him anywhere, which meant he went to work the next morning still irritated with Diane and Jeffrey, and with Sloane. Maybe even more than them he was irritated with himself, because upon her refusal of his help, he'd sounded almost accusatory when he'd asked if her rejection had anything to do with the man in the slick suit she'd been standing with at the food hall.

Her blank look more annoyed than appeased him.

That's when he'd realized this weird jealousy made him not at all rational. Or agreeable.

It was making him downright moody, as a matter of fact, despite Sloane telling him that guy who'd seemed so attentive in the pizza line was her coworker. Her *married* coworker.

Of course, the moodiness might have another source altogether—work-related. There was a shortage on his order of mulch, a virus was dominoing through the front office staff, and they'd found a glitch in the accounting software. The long hours— dawn to midnight—necessary to overcome all that meant he didn't have an opportunity to check in with Sloane and Paige for two days, though he knew they'd been spending time with those out-of-town grandparents.

The forced separation from his house guests took his mood even lower, so when he received a call from Molly on Wednesday afternoon, he immediately jumped to dire conclusions. "Who's hurt?" he demanded. "How bad is it?"

"Great to hear your voice too," she said, sounding disgustingly jovial, given that one of her sisters had lost a major limb or perhaps developed a Pacific Northwestern disease.

Then his heart stopped as a new notion occurred to him. "Did someone elope today?"

"I'm sure someone did," Molly said, still in that

good-natured tone, "in this great wide world of ours."

Eli pinched the bridge of his nose. "What's going on? Don't make me nuts."

"That might be us," Molly said, "given we haven't heard from you since the weekend. We started worrying that you might have been consumed by a previously undetected black mold infestation at the house."

"Bite your tongue." But he couldn't believe he'd gone so long without talking to them. "Be serious now. Everybody's okay?"

"Yes. We're hiking and eating and eating and hiking, just as planned. Also, we took some ferries for more hiking and eating."

"All right then."

"And you? Seriously, Eli, we're worried. We called the front desk at King's and heard about some virus barreling through everyone there. You're not sick?"

"I'm good."

"Are you eating? You need food, you know, and—"

"Sloane's been leaving me meals in the refrigerator." *Uh-oh*, he thought, the instant that spilled from his mouth.

*"Sloane?"*

Shit. Shit shit shit. "Didn't I say?" he asked, casual as can be.

"Say what, exactly?"

"She's run into some trouble." If it wouldn't have made a detectable noise, he might have thumped his head against his desk. "Trouble" was the custody thing, because that was at the forefront of his mind, but it wasn't a topic to share with the girls.

"Regarding her, uh, roof."

"She has roof trouble and you have home-cooked meals in the refrigerator?"

"Yeah. Well." He hauled in a silent breath, let it out. "She and Paige and Boo are living at our house. Just for a few more days."

Molly's ensuing silence was long and loaded. "You're living with Sloane and her daughter?"

"They're living with me. And the dog. He needed a dry place to stay. One with electricity."

"Because Boo likes to read himself to sleep at night." There was a return of good humor to his sister's voice. "I remember that about him."

"It's just for a few more days," he repeated, and his dark mood turned downright foul.

*A few more days.* That phrase kept echoing in his head past the ending of the call and until dusk and beyond, as he worked past closing and late into the nighttime hours once again. When he finally drove to the house, he imagined Sloane and Paige would already be abed and he'd rattle around the kitchen for a beer and a snack then head to the TV to watch alone for a couple of hours, already a lifestyle that had become monotonous over the past nights.

Ironic, wasn't it? He chafed at the quiet without the rest of the family traipsing through, when quiet was all he'd been dreaming about, it seemed, for years. But he'd feel differently in a different location, he assured himself as he pulled into the garage.

Once he moved. He'd find some condo complex popular with single adults. There, he'd share a wall or two with a stranger and so be alone but not lonely with the droning noise of their television set or the rattle-bang-moan of their sex life keeping him company.

What a treat.

He pushed into the kitchen, noting the light over the range had been left on. Sloane did that—made sure he came into the house with some kind of welcome.

This time it was accompanied by a scream.

His heart shot to his throat and adrenaline spiked his bloodstream. He dropped his jacket to the floor and his keys too, then he was sprinting up the stairs, his blood chilled by yet another shriek.

He almost collided with Sloane in the hallway outside the closed door to Paige's room. They pushed through as a unit, stumbling in their haste. In the glow of a night-light, the child sat straight up, the covers at her waist, Boo standing at the foot of the bed whining.

Eli snapped his fingers to get the dog's attention and the animal bounded off the mattress to rub against his legs. He stroked his hand over the canine's head, calming it, as Sloane tried calming the girl. She sat the on the edge of the bed and attempted pulling Paige into her arms, but the wide-eyed child was about as bendable as a board, her breath sawing in an out while resisting the move into her mother's embrace with thrashing arms and legs.

"Paige," Sloane called. "*Paige.*"

The child moaned in distress, her face flushed and sweaty.

Eli couldn't stand by any longer. He approached the bed and kneeled on the floor, his hand running over the little girl's damp hair. "Paige. Buddy. You're okay. We're all here."

Her head swiveled his way, and then she jerked, as if awakening. Her mouth rounded, clearly in preparation for another scream, but it died on her lips, coming out as a wilted whimper. Then she flung herself toward her mother and began weeping.

His heart broke at the inconsolable crying. When the girls were hurt physically or emotionally, he'd had to steel himself against their tears every single time. It was no less taxing now, actually worse, as Sloane's distressed gaze lifted to his. He shifted so he could wrap his arms around both mother and child. He held them, rocking a little, trying to soothe all of them as his eyes closed and he pressed his lips to the top of Paige's hair and then to the top of Sloane's.

Boo crowded in, his doggy head bumping Eli's shoulder. "Good boy," he murmured. "You're going to be okay too."

Later, when Paige had dropped into an exhausted sleep and Boo was once again watching over her, Eli followed Sloane from the room. Her pale appearance didn't reassure him much, though she told him she'd read of such events happening to children.

"Night terrors," she said, coming to stop in the doorway to her own room.

Bad dreams had visited the King household on occasion, but nothing as dramatic as this. "Should she see a doctor?"

"If they become frequent, but she'll likely not remember this in the morning and maybe never have another."

He pulled in a long breath and then pushed his hands through his hair. "I feel a few years older."

She smiled again. "I know what you mean—and thanks for the help, by the way."

"I didn't do anything," he grumbled. "Usually after a night event I spend a solid fifteen minutes ensuring no monsters are under the bed, in the closets, or tucked into the drawers. Somewhere I have a bottle of anti-beast and brute spray—my own special recipe, by the way. A little water and lemon juice. But Paige drifted off without all that."

"It's not the same as a nightmare."

"Do you know what causes it?"

Shrugging, Sloane looked away. "Change in routine, perhaps. Stress."

The arrival of poaching grandparents. "Sloane—"

"I'm managing, Eli. You'll see."

Oh, yeah. He *would* see, he vowed to himself. That low mood of his had been due to frustration and unfamiliar helplessness. But now he had a new determination, born out of those moments of holding mother and child in his arms. No matter what it took, he would see that these two vulnerable people living under his roof didn't suffer from anxiety or worry like this again.

Surely he could do that without compromising his future and his freedom.

Sloane pointed the remote at the television and searched for a program that would distract her from the knowledge that, with the exception of Boo, she was alone in the house. He lay snoring beside the family room couch while she tried appreciating the relative silence.

As it was poker night, Eli had gone straight from work to the home of whomever was hosting this week's game. Paige, after a few daily outings with her grandparents during which Sloane acted as chaperone, was spending the night with them by herself. She'd seemed happy enough with the idea, buoyed by the carrot of spending time in the hot tub at the house the Dunlaps' were short-term renting.

While Sloane had struggled with the idea of letting Paige out of her sight until morning, she'd decided it was a sound tactic. Perhaps Diane wouldn't push for more if Sloane didn't object to her daughter being alone in the grandparents' company.

During her first solo hour she'd occupied herself with packing her and Paige's things. Alice and Joe had returned from their vacation that day, and she'd filled them in on the situation at the cottage. They'd been apologetic and promised to help find a long-term solution, but immediately invited she and Paige to move in with them.

A tempting offer. And she was prepared to take them up on it at a moment's notice, since she'd boxed their belongings. But introducing yet another change into Paige's life right now seemed unwise and then there was, well…Eli.

This would be Sloane's final opportunity to be close to the man she loved and walking out of his life took more strength than she had at the moment. To her mind, his sisters' return would be a natural breaking point. The Kings would have their house to themselves again and Sloane would move on.

For the next few days, though, she'd keep her feelings for Eli secret while secretly enjoying sharing her little family's life with him.

She tuned to a nature documentary that wasn't of the lions-eating-zebras variety, but one about the hidden life of orchids. The narrator's voice soothed her and the visuals were restful. Lost in green leaves and creamy petals, she almost missed the groaning of the automatic garage door opening. But it caught Boo's attention, and he was on his feet, shaking himself so his collar and tags jingled as Eli strolled into the family room from the kitchen.

At the sight of him, her heart performed a swoop-dive, its new normal. She drank him in, the long hair, the long body, the way his gaze sought her out and warmed when their eyes met. "Hey." The dog rushed him and she watched his long fingers fondle Boo's ears, flushing as she recalled the sensation of his touch, the calluses on his palms gently abrading the curve of her hips or the undersides of her breasts. To hide the way her nipples reacted to the memories, she drew up her knees to her chest, her stocking feet braced on the seat cushion.

Eli crossed to sit beside her, taking up the remote to thumb down the volume. "Paige sleeping okay?"

"She's spending the night with Diane and Jeffrey."

He raised a brow. "Yeah?"

Sloane half-turned to better face him. "I don't want them to be able to say I keep their granddaughter from them. And Paige seemed enthusiastic. Milkshakes may have been mentioned."

"Ah." He slid down on the cushions, resting his head as if suddenly weary.

"You're back sooner than I expected. Did you win everyone's money?"

He snorted. "Another run of bad luck. So I ducked out for an early, peaceful night."

"Oh." She unfolded her body, started to rise. "I'll go upstairs so you can enjoy—"

Eli grabbed her arm, staying her movement.

"You're peaceful. Stay and watch some TV with me."

Powerless to deny him, Sloane settled back. Boo took to his place with a satisfied doggy sound and the orchid documentary droned on. At first hyperaware of the man sitting so close by—her skin tingled and her pulse jumped at his every shift and breath—soon enough she felt herself drift as her eyelids grew heavy.

Hypnotized, she thought on a half-giddy, half-drowsy thought, by Eli's warmth, the hint of his scent in the air, the...the sense of him beside her. His companionship.

Sometime later, she roused. Opening her eyes to slits, she noted the documentary was no longer about orchids, but butterflies, or maybe that was her stomach fluttering as she realized that she and her host had become tangled. They each lay on their sides, Eli's body spooning hers, both pairs of their legs curled so they could fit on two-thirds of the cushions. Boo had made a place for himself on the other third.

A groggy thought emerged, *bad dog*, but it floated away when Eli's arm—the one banding her middle—flexed, drawing her closer to him. She put her hand over his to entwine their fingers, only partly conscious of that action's dangers.

*Don't give away your secret*, she thought, then drifted away again.

The trill of her phone jolted her out of sleep.

She blinked, tried moving, but was hampered by that heavy arm. When her phone rang out again, with more effort she pushed herself to a sitting position and untangled her fingers from Eli's. Behind her he signaled sleepy disapproval, but she ignored him to snatch up her cell from the coffee table.

Diane Dunlap. On a quick breath, she answered.

"Yes? What's happened?"

"Nothing to worry about," Diane said in a brusque tone. "Paige woke up and insists on speaking with you."

"Yes, of course," Sloane replied. "Put her on."

"Mommy?" Paige's voice sounded small.

"What's up, baby?"

"I want you. Can you come get me?"

Before she had a chance to reply, Diane's voice came through the device—she'd obviously taken back the phone. "That's not necessary, Sloane. Paige will be just fine if you wish her good night again and tell her you'll see her in the morning."

"I don't mind coming to get her," Sloane said. "I think—"

"It's not *necessary*, Sloane," the older woman asserted. "Paige is a big girl and will be just fine until tomorrow."

In the background, Sloane could hear her daughter ask to talk to her mommy again. "Put Paige back on, please, Diane."

"Really, Sloane—"

"Please put Paige back on."

Her daughter sounded sniffly now. "Mommy?"

"I'm on my way, sweet girl. You collect Bun and hold onto it until I'm there. It won't be long." With a warm goodbye, she ended the call before Diane could object again.

Eli was sitting up beside her now, alert-eyed, his focus on her. "What's going on?"

"Paige wants to come home." The words popped out before she realized their implication. "I mean, um, she wants me."

"Then let's get her you," Eli said, jumping to his

feet.

"You don't need to—"

"Your car has Paige's seat," he said, ignoring her protest. "Grab your keys."

Boo tagged along so Sloane had an entourage when she approached the front door of the seaside vacation rental. The porch light glowed and Diane already stood in the open doorway, Jeffrey hovering behind her.

"Sloane," the older woman said in a disapproving tone. "To disturb the child's night like this—"

"The child's night was already disturbed," Eli said from behind her. His hand landed on Sloane's shoulder.

Diane's attention shifted to the man behind Sloane. "Eli King," she said, her frosty tone thawing somewhat. "It's good to see you despite the circumstances."

Before he could respond, Paige pushed between the Dunlaps. "Mommy!" Her joy was palpable and she launched herself forward, causing Sloane to go back on one foot to keep her balance. She bumped into Eli, his body solid as a rock, and his free hand settled on her other shoulder.

With his warm weight behind her, Sloane shifted her daughter to hold her close. "Thank you, Diane, Jeffrey. We'll be in touch tomorrow."

"No," Diane said, her face suddenly contorting. "Don't do this. Don't ruin this one too!"

Sloane froze. "What?"

"You ruined JJ," the older woman said. "I don't want you to damage his daughter as well."

Behind her, Eli's body stiffened. "What the hell?" he murmured.

Jeffrey winced. "Diane. Stop."

"I won't stop," she exclaimed. "I won't stop because Paige belongs with us. With Jeffrey and me."

There it was. Out in the open. Sloane went white-hot and a high whine sounded in her ears. Her mouth dried and she began to shake. "I'm n-not to blame for JJ's choices."

"Who else then?" Diane cried. She crossed her arms, defiant and angry. "And I won't lose someone else I love. I won't."

Jeffrey put his arm around her. "Diane—"

"We've contacted a lawyer." The older woman eyes held a militant light now. "We're going to sue you for custody."

"We're not going to sue," Jeffrey said. "Sloane, yes, we talked to a lawyer—"

"This is nuts," Eli said, stepping from behind Sloane so they stood shoulder-to-shoulder. "You're not going to threaten this mother and daughter with a lawyer, with talk of taking custody, or with anything close to it."

Diane narrowed her eyes at Eli now. "She's *my* granddaughter. Don't you understand that? *Mine.*"

Sloane, until that moment half-paralyzed by shock and fear at the accusation, came completely alive again. With the weight of her child in her arms, with Paige's wet tears clinging to her neck, she took her own step forward. "That's enough, Diane," she said firmly. Decisively. "You're upsetting Paige."

The woman's eyes narrowed. "You—"

"Yes, me. I'm a person, Diane. Not an obstacle or an adversary. I'm the mother of your granddaughter and there is nothing, *nothing*, I won't do for her."

"There's nothing I won't do to have her," Diane

said tightly. "You fight me and—"

"I will fight you." Sloane thought of Eli raising four little girls alone and her courage soared. He'd prevailed against difficulty and uncertainty and so could she.

"And you will lose if you take it that far," she continued, her conviction ringing in her voice. Even she could hear it. One woman's bitterness and selfishness was nothing against Sloane's love and determination. "Believe me. If you try this, you will lose everything you claim to hold so dear."

With that, she spun and marched to her car, Paige held firmly in her arms, Eli at her back, Boo eager to dispense doggy kisses to his human sister once they made it inside the vehicle.

Her daughter and her entourage safe.

Back at Eli's, Paige once again in Sloane's embrace, all of them tromped up the stairs on the way to the little girl's room. Her daughter didn't protest as Sloane tucked her into bed with Bun the bunny and when Paige asked for Baby Sally, Eli found the doll and slipped her under the covers as well. Boo jumped up on the bed, circled down, and then it was time for the three regulation kisses.

By the third, the little girl appeared already fast asleep.

Somehow Eli had Sloane's hand as they went out the door. He continued holding it all the way down the stairs and as he led her into his room. Sloane put up no protest.

"I'd just like to hold you," he murmured, drawing her toward the bed. "I just need to hold you."

Sloane felt buffeted and bruised and remembering the contentment and peace she'd felt earlier in his arms, she went into them again, this time grateful and wholly aware. They stood in each other's embrace for long moments, but then it wasn't enough. He reached for the hem of her T-shirt, her fingers found the button of his jeans and unfastened it despite their fine tremors.

Then they were naked and on the sheets and it was not like their previous encounters. Now the fire of passion was banked, but it burned hot at the center, a steady pulse. She kissed his jaw and he kissed her throat. She stroked his belly and he caressed her breast.

They explored unhurried as if each touch was a healing wand to take away the slings and arrows of the day, the grief of the past, the uncertainty of the future. Eli slid down her body, peppering her with stinging kisses she hoped she'd feel forever and she opened to him, her legs splaying wide to offer him the center of her.

To offer him everything.

His mouth fed on her wet flesh like he needed sustenance, his fingers firm on her hips as she writhed against his clever tongue. He lifted his head, taking a look at her with drowsy eyes. "How can you be so sweet?" he asked, but didn't wait for an answer before he went back to long, luscious licks and deep delves. She clutched his hair, not sure if she could handle another second of this pleasure-torture.

"Please," she said, tugging. "I want your mouth on mine."

He stilled, his big, strong shoulders keeping her legs splayed and what should be obscene felt so personal, so intimate, her heart climbed into her throat. Then he began to move, and the wet of her on his lips tracked up her belly and her chest, the scent of her arousal on him more of an aphrodisiac than…

She couldn't think of anything more arousing.

Until he kissed her, her spicy-salty-sweet flavor on his tongue making her moan. She rolled, taking him beneath her, and he let out a small laugh-grunt, and then she was on top, grinning down at him. Playful, in the midst of the intensely personal.

Because she trusted him, she thought. Eli King, the eradicator of beasts and brutes, who had showed her his vulnerable side too.

His fear of Baby Sally.

His grief over the death of his parents.

The anger that had him sitting on rooftops and shouting at stars.

Like her, he had his own bruises that needed treating.

So she offered her best medicine, with drawn-out kisses and long strokes of her hands. She played with his balls, crawling down his body to take them into her mouth, tonguing them until he called for mercy. Then she paid attention to his shaft and crown, sucking and stroking until his fingers flexed in her hair and she was drawn up to meet his lips again.

"I've never had it so good," he whispered, causing tears to sting in her eyes. She bit the side of his throat and he groaned then guided her head to his left pectoral. "Here," he said, his voice guttural. "Mark me here."

So she did, understanding he wanted proof of this, that they'd come together for pleasure and for this deep connection. They were tender and rough in turn—he closed his teeth around her nipple then sucked it with soft lips and tongue. She firmly squeezed his swollen member and he bucked into her hand even as she pressed a long, gentle kiss to his lips.

Then he turned her to her side and he was behind her, spooning her like they'd been on the couch earlier in the night. Sex in this position was new to Sloane, and she arched her back, pushing her bottom into his groin to hear him moan. He lifted her thigh over his, opening her, and then he slipped inside, his condom-covered erection bumping over her clit and then sliding over sensitive tissues to find her opening. He pressed in, she pressed back, trying to take more of him, but this angle kept penetration shallow.

Still, it was delicious, and he added to it by sliding one hand beneath her so he could play with her nipple, thumbing and squeezing. His other hand slid down her belly to caress her folds and then toy with her clit. He circled and rubbed as his shallow dives became deeper lunges. It required concentration to take as much of him as she could with each thrust, opening her body to him, opening herself to a new experience.

His front was damp against her back and he buried his head in her neck, murmuring praise and nonsense words and dirty things that made her heart race and her skin flash hot.

"Yeah, that's good, take me deep," he said. "I'm going to fill you so full you won't forget me for a week."

She'd never forget him.

"God, so tight. So hot." His teeth worried her earlobe and she could feel him throbbing inside her, or maybe that was her heart, or lust, or just wanting, greedy need.

"Make me come," she moaned. *Make me yours.*

He rushed in on a groan, his forehead to her neck, his body heated steel behind her, inside her, heat surrounding her, Eli.

Eli at her back, her partner in this ferocious, beautiful moment.

Her excitement climbed and she fed it bit and pieces, his scent, the look of his hand cupping her breast, the feel of his groin against her bottom, the dominance of male penetration. On his next lunge, her breath held and she poised on the edge of it, on the edge of what she wanted most.

He bit her neck, he pinched her clit.

And as he groaned his own release, she shattered, a thousand swirling pieces, but all held within the circle of the arms of Eli. Slayer of hearts.

As the waves receded, she turned her face into his bicep and mouthed the words that wanted to burst from her. "I love you," she said silently, blissful and triumphant that her secret had remained just that.

# Chapter 13

Eli woke with the light of a gray dawn silvering his bedroom. For a moment he didn't move, his body heavy with leftover sexual satiety and his mind humming with satisfaction. The solution had come to him in his sleep. He had it all figured out.

Underscoring his good mood was the fact that Sloane had not left his bed. Unlike their other encounters, when she'd scurried upstairs while it was still dark, today he was greeting the morning with her beside him, her naked body sprawled on her stomach, her head turned his way. He stared into her sleeping face, noting her kiss-swollen lips and flushed cheeks. With her curly hair mussed she looked debauched…and delectable.

Innocence corrupted.

And optimism saved, if the plan his subconscious had hatched overnight worked—and it would. It might not be the romantic happy-ever-after she so wanted to believe in—*somebody gets to have that*, she'd once said, as almost a plea—but it would guarantee an ending that both mother and daughter deserved.

He smiled to himself, thinking he couldn't ask for a better conclusion to his bachelor spring break. Though it wasn't exactly what he'd sought as he'd waved his sisters on their adventure, he wasn't going to complain about the sex...or the warm, beautiful, valiant woman who had unexpectedly come with it.

As he watched, Sloane's eyes fluttered open. They widened slightly at her first glimpse of him, then they squeezed shut again and he almost laughed at her transparent attempt to pretend away the fact she'd spent the entire night in his bed.

"Think about it like this," he suggested. "I'll get up first and make *you* coffee."

She remained unmoving. "I didn't intend to sleep this late," she said in a husky voice that caused his dick to twitch. *Hmm.* Maybe not so sated.

"It was a rough night." In more ways than one. First, the confrontation with Paige's grandparents, and then the ardent and extended tumble in his bed, the manner and mood of it swinging wildly between tempestuous and tender. Anyone might not be at their sharpest come morning.

Except Eli. He felt energized and downright eager to face the day.

"Paige is still asleep?"

The monitor stood on his bedside table. "Seems so," he said, "which gives me time and opportunity to present to you my clever plan."

He sat up, and so did Sloane, her hand pressing the sheet to her bare breasts. "What kind of plan?

Why do I need a plan? Why do I need a *clever* plan?"

So damn wary. He frowned, disliking this notion that she was always looking for a catch, that she always expected things to be harder rather than easier. "You need to see more evidence of things going your way," he said.

She drew back a little, a crease between her brows. "And you're going to show me that evidence?"

"Damn straight." He swung his legs over the side of the bed, reaching for the pajama pants slung over the straight chair beside the bedside table. He pulled them on, then tossed the flannel shirt he'd worn the night before in her direction.

In another context, his idea could be delivered naked, but now he thought she'd appreciate being decently covered. With six long strides, he reached the tall antique dresser against one wall, and used the small key on the dish there to unlock a narrow top drawer. He fished out a square jewelry box, the maroon velvet covering worn with age.

Then he turned toward Sloane, her beautiful eyes on him, her expression puzzled, her shoulders and chest enveloped by his shirt.

She might as well have been wearing satin and lace. His mind spun off on a brief fantasy of it, Sloane in a creation from that high-end lingerie catalog that he'd recently found in the mail. She'd have the time and leisure to tempt some man with the seductive outfit, the beginning to a sunlit or starlit escapade unbound by real world limitations or responsibilities.

He wanted to give that to the woman right now in his bed—something he more than suspected the single mom had never afforded or allowed herself.

His fingers closed around the velvet ring box.

This would have to do.

Approaching her, he watched her try to tame her mussed hair with her fingers, her watchful gaze trained on his face and not on what he held. "I'm thinking," he said, then flipped open the box to reveal the white gold band and the simple diamond at its center, "that we announce we're engaged."

She jumped, eyes rounding. "What?"

"We announce we're engaged." He tilted the box to give her a better view of its contents.

Her glance flicked down, and she recoiled, as if spying a snake. "What is *that*?"

"My grandmother's ring. We can size it to fit you if need be."

She stared at him, her expression aghast. Maybe it seemed an odd offer, to permanently adjust the heirloom for a temporary alliance, but not to him. Above all things, Eli wanted Sloane feeling secure, for once with her feet squarely on a solid foundation such as he'd always had...and perhaps too often taken for granted.

"Eli," she spoke slowly. "I don't understand."

"It's simple," he said, sitting on the edge of the bed. "The Dunlaps will back off if we present a united front. You know I'm right about that. So today we'll tell a little white lie and declare we're engaged. Then they continue their visit to the area with or without contact with Paige—your call, of course. When they return to Florida..."

"What then?"

He shrugged. "We return to our pre-spring break lives."

She looked at him, her expression noncommittal. "And I return your ring for the day when you find the woman you truly want to marry."

*Hmm.* That part he hadn't thought through. Would some future female object to jewelry he'd already given to another woman? No matter. He didn't see himself with anyone else.

Right now.

Before he had a chance to communicate that, Sloane had scrambled out of the bed. His shirt tails fluttered around her thighs as she flitted about the room scooping up the pieces of her wardrobe that had been thrown off the night before. "We won't be doing that," she said, brisk and businesslike.

Frowning, he crossed his arms over his chest. "We won't be doing…what?"

Her blue eyes turned stony. "Any of that."

At the rejection of his grand plan, that crap mood he'd battled for days descended swiftly. "And why exactly not?" he asked, insulted.

"It would be bad for me."

His mouth dropped. "Are you kidding? It would be good for you. And Paige. We'd be doing this *for* you."

"You mean you'd be sacrificing that swinging bachelorhood you've been dreaming about for more than a decade on my behalf. I don't need rescuing, Eli."

Well, of course she needed rescuing. Wasn't it obvious? And rescuing was what he was pretty damn good at, if the many batches of beast-and-brute spray he'd mixed over the years meant anything. "I'm only trying to help."

"I don't need your charity." Clothes were clutched to her chest, an armor, he could tell. "And I see that I've given you the wrong idea about that by moving in. I'm sorry I took advantage of you."

"Took advantage of me?" Now he was getting really pissed. She made it sound like he was some mark. Like he was some...some fool. "You cleaned, you did laundry, you cooked me meals."

Sloane threw out a hand. "I prepared food."

"You helped me get over my fear of dolls."

"Baby Sally still makes you shake in your boots."

True. But... "You brought life into this house, you and Paige and Boo, when it walked out with my sisters."

"You *wanted* to be alone."

He ignored that, because it turned out alone wasn't all that it was cracked up to be...instead of feeling liberated, he'd felt, fuck it, lonely. "You're good company. You made me laugh and you listened to me and you...shit, Sloane, I've never had sex so good."

Her flushed face told him he'd found a weak spot. "That's not a basis for an engagement."

"We're getting *fake* engaged," he pointed out. "So there's no reason to get all prickly and stubborn about it."

"There's one reason to get prickly and stubborn," she countered, vehement, then she sighed and her voice softened. "I...I don't want anything fake with you, Eli."

"For God's sake, it's for a greater good," he started, feeling uneasy because she was edging for the door and he thought he was about to lose her. A dark premonition told him it might not be a temporary loss.

Sloane put one hand on the doorknob. "You know," she said, sighing again. "I want to get angry, I want to accuse you of insensitivity and rail at you for your white knight tendencies."

He huffed. "I'm no—"

"I want to tell you I see that you've been using your business and your sisters as a reason not to live a full life, one that includes a romantic partner. They're your excuse. You use them as a defense against more potential grief because you were so hurt when those you loved left you."

A muscle ticked in his jaw. "They died."

"To you, they left."

Stung, he threw the ring box to the bed. "And you're so different? Four years of celibacy, remember?"

"Four years raising a child and trying to keep us financially afloat."

Yeah, he saw that. Admired it, even. But he wasn't feeling reasonable right now. "Again, how's that any different than me?"

Her fingers turned the knob. "Because I've managed to fall in love, and that's despite never having been loved myself, not once."

He stared at her. What was she talking about? Who did she fall for? That colleague from the food hall? Some other—

"With you, Eli," Sloane said gently. "I'm in love with you."

His knees folded and his ass dropped to the bed.

"And I don't want to pretend it away any longer or enter in any kind of pretend relationship," she continued. "Not when I know, after my time here with you, what a real, solid romantic partnership could be like."

It was past his turn to talk, but speech was beyond him.

She smiled a little, as if she knew. "So thank you, Eli King, for showing me that. And for making me sure I want and deserve to be loved."

And with that, she was gone.

Stunned and dismayed, he remained on the bed a while longer and then stumbled into the shower, standing under the hot spray as he tried to grapple with what she'd said and how he felt about it. The woman's words had blindsided him and yet…and yet…

And yet his emotions were so damn mixed he couldn't keep a single thought in his head. Instead, fragments of conversation drifted in—*I'm in love with you. You've been using your business and your sisters as a reason not to live a full life*—then slid out again, to be replaced by a myriad of Sloane-expressions, bliss, bewilderment, hurt. *I don't want anything fake with you, Eli.*

That's what he'd offered a beautiful, resolute woman who took on life still wearing a smile, though it had knocked her down one time, two times, three…he'd proposed a phony relationship to that wonderful woman who'd been sharing his bed.

What a fucking prince.

Angry at himself, at her for pointing up just what a misstep he'd made, he emerged from his bedroom, instantly aware the first floor was empty. So he stalked up the stairs, hoping that upon confronting her the chaos in his head would clear and he'd say…

That was the issue—he didn't know his next step.

But once on the upper landing, he sensed a vacancy there, too. He strode first to the room Sloane had used, at the far end of the hall. No sign of her or her belongings.

Paige's room was devoid of her presence as well. The bed was neatly made and the toys in the playroom put away. Bookshelves in order. No Boo.

Not even a stray dog hair or any sign of Baby Sally.

That's when he realized Sloane must have been prepared to leave him. Surely just yesterday there'd been a jumble of books and doll clothes on the rose-patterned rug. The bed's coverlet had been rumpled and the pillow askew. Now all was in order...as if Paige and Boo and Sloane had never been there.

Fine. Okay. That made today so much easier, right? That made getting back to his pre-spring break life a much simpler thing.

Turning, he began to leave, then his gaze snagged on the pencil marks on the doorjamb. Nora, Allison, Lynnie, Molly, a graphic sign of the passage of years. His head lowered and he glanced at the spot where he'd measured Paige, his finger on the wood at the level of the crown of her head. Though he'd made no indication with ink or lead, he saw it as if he had, as if words had been written.

*Paige was here.*

*Boo was here.*

*Sloane was here.*

But all three had gone and left him. Like his sisters would go someday, leaving this house eternally empty. His gut clenched and a surge of cold certainty rushed through him, pushing out other emotions. Staring at the doorjamb, he knew what must be done.

It was a matter of minutes to collect the small pry bar from the garage. Then he was in the doorway of the playroom again. The next people to live in this place wouldn't want the old toys, the old books, the old memories.

They assaulted him then, little girls swirling through his memory like ghosts clamoring for his attention—to check their homework, to braid their hair, to can-you-believe what their friend Amy/Nicole/Jessica/Teagan had said. Always standing between him and the freedom most men of his age experienced.

Little girls who'd brought to his life laughter and order. Who gave it meaning.

Who'd kept him so busy he'd never fully dealt with the loss of his mother and father.

*You use them as a defense against more potential grief because you were so hurt when those you loved left you.*

Where the fuck were his sisters now when he needed some distraction from this new pain?

As if in answer, he heard the lock of the front door give and the telltale squeal of its hinges. For a second, he wondered if his house guests had returned, but then familiar voices sounded and familiar footsteps clattered up the stairs.

A familiar figure stood in the hallway, finding him with tool in hand. She eyed that, eyed him. "You guys!" Molly yelled without taking her gaze off him. "He's up here!"

Then Peanut Shell joined Peanut—or was it the other way around?—and it cut to realize the King siblings would never know the real story behind that joke. They'd never know all the stories that belonged to their parents. They only had each other—and the family folklore they'd created on their own.

All four sisters were staring at him now. Then they were looking at the pry bar and then the doorjamb, each one of them so damn clever.

"I wasn't going to do anything," he said, feeling guilty, as if he were the naughty child caught red-handed. But it was true, he wouldn't have harmed that innocent piece of wood.

The next owners would have to take care of it. Paint and brush perhaps, or—

Shit. He looked down at the tool. Could he save that piece of wood with those measurements somehow, detaching it from the rest of the trim without causing damage?

"Put the weapon down," Nora called out, smirking at him, "and back away slowly."

Right. A problem for another day.

Walking toward his siblings, he addressed their surprise, early arrival. "What's this about, girls? Is the car wrecked? Were you run out of town by a jealous girlfriend? Did Allison finally admit she can't sleep without that boy band night-light she's had for a decade?"

Then the sisters were upon him, hugging, chattering, exclaiming, their voices echoing in his head and off the walls of this house that warmed with their presence. They provided an excellent diversion and he was caught up in the maelstrom of their return. A pile of their luggage appeared in the front entrance and the washer and dryer began a vigorous workout. The four expressed surprise at the foodstuffs in the pantry and were in near-shock over the leftovers in the fridge that didn't come in take-out boxes.

Not until dinner, when they all sat around the table eating from the lasagna and the chicken broccoli casseroles left by his house guest, did he hear about the blow-by-blow details of their vacation. They tripped all over each other in describing their adventures and he laughed and grimaced and expressed big-brother concern when appropriate. It felt like old times, good times, and he relaxed in his chair, sipping beer and pretending to himself that all was well.

Returned to normal.

Then four pairs of clever King gazes fixed on him and Lynnie asked the first leading question, making clear it was his turn to talk. So he told them about his two weeks—a stripped-down version. Before, he'd mentioned the neighbor's roof issue and that Sloane and company had moved into the house to Molly, but he explained the necessity again. And then…Christ, and then he was confiding more. Not all, not everything Sloane had admitted to that morning, but Eli told his sisters about his offer of a temporary engagement as a way to put a damper on the scheming grandparents who thought to take Sloane's daughter from her.

"She refused you?" Allison said, and he didn't know which part of what he'd spilled had caused her eyebrows to climb halfway to her hairline.

"Yeah." He pushed his plate aside. "And the way things were left between us… I suppose I'm telling you this because if we meet again, there might be awkwardness."

"How's that?" Molly asked.

"She didn't appreciate—" He broke off, and looked around the table. "Am I so wrong for wanting to make things easier for her?"

They didn't have an answer to his demand.

Later, Nora found him in the family room, brooding on the couch, something playing on the TV as background noise. She slid a wrapped present onto the coffee table in front of him.

"I found this in the linen closet."

"Oh."

"It bears your distinctive wrapping style."

She meant the bow was crooked. Over ten years of packaging gifts for birthdays and holidays and he'd still not mastered ribbon. "It's Paige's birthday party tomorrow."

"Lynnie and Molly were invited," Nora said. "How about you?"

"The birthday girl asked me herself."

His sister settled onto the couch beside him. "You should go."

"Sloane called me a white knight," Eli said, shaking his head. "And not in a good way."

Nora smiled a little. "Is that right?"

"She claims she doesn't want to be rescued."

"I suppose your offer of a temporary...alliance felt patronizing."

"Is that a crack about being old again?" he asked, narrowing his eyes.

"No." She laughed. "But I can see how those white knights seemed annoyingly noble on their high horses."

"You're mixing metaphors."

"Am I?" Nora asked. "Those guys rode above the fray in all that protective armor. Never risking, you know, their hearts."

*Above the fray. Protective armor. Never risking their hearts.* Eli stared at her. "I'm afraid of you."

She laughed again. "You should at least go to Paige's party. It will clarify things...and probably clear that bad taste from your mouth."

He opened it to protest, but he could see she was right. One, he couldn't disappoint the birthday girl who had invited him herself, and two, he didn't feel like ducking Sloane for the rest of his life. Eli King, as the last years had proven, was no coward.

And clearing the bad taste from his mouth wouldn't be a bad thing.

"How'd you get to be so smart?" he asked Nora.

"I was raised by the best."

He smiled. "Mom and Dad would be happy to hear that."

Nora just looked at him, then kicked him in the leg with a bare foot. "I'm talking about you, idiot. I haven't forgotten a thing that I learned from you."

After everyone had gone to bed, what she'd said kept running through his head. He stared at his bedroom ceiling for a long while and sleepless, finally got up to do something he hadn't in years. Being as quiet as he could, he made his way to the roof. There, he took a seat and stared upward, waiting for the anger to rise. This time he meant to embrace it, to experience it fully, to—he hoped—let it finally burn out.

But instead of finding himself silently shouting at the stars like he used to, he breathed deeply of the cold night air. Instead of heated emotion leaving him, a cool calm entered him, a sense of approval, and a self-knowledge that he'd done well. That in doing the best he could, he'd managed to keep them all solid, centered, together.

At last, he made a promise to his parents—to cherish family and to maintain those connections he'd forged with his sisters even as their lives moved on. And then he vowed, under those same stars that had been silent witnesses to the anger and anguish of his younger years, to always appreciate what was most important in life.

*I haven't forgotten a thing I learned from you.*

The birthday party had gone well, Sloane thought, as she gathered torn wrapping paper and the remnants of the delicious strawberry shortcake cupcakes. The guests continued to enjoy themselves and the satisfied glow from that warmed the coldness in her belly that had settled in when she walked out of Eli's house the day before.

She'd billed the move to Alice and Joe's as a pre-birthday treat for Paige and her daughter had accepted it easily enough. Excitement over the party had done the rest. Sloane didn't even think the little girl understood yet that Eli was missing from their life. When his sisters, Lynnie and Molly, had arrived on scene, Sloane hadn't witnessed the birthday girl asking about him anyway.

For herself, she'd been using her hostess duties as a reason to keep her distance from the pair, other than a smile and a wave. She'd exchanged friendly conversation with Rona and her husband, and the subject of Paige's grandparents had been avoided on both sides.

The grassy park bordered the beach and ocean and Sloane had reserved a collection of picnic tables under an open-sided, metal-roofed shelter. Parents of the little ones invited had showed up late morning with scooters and trikes to take advantage of the cement pathways and some of their group had even walked their kids to the surf to ankle-wade in the chilly Pacific.

She leaned down to pick up a paper-wrapped candy that had escaped the piñata, then jerked sharply upright at an exuberant shriek. Her gaze found Paige, who was running full-tilt toward the tall figure of a man strolling over the grass in their direction.

As she watched, her daughter shouted, "E!" and launched herself into Eli's arms.

For a moment, Sloane froze, then she forced herself to move, knowing she needed to intervene, if only to save her child from strengthening an ill-fated attachment. Moving forward felt like walking through a sea of the icing that had tasted so delicious on the birthday treats. It slowed her footsteps and weighed her entire body down, but she slogged on all the same, even as her eyes met Eli's.

In that instant, a change transformed his face.

A moment before he'd been focused on Paige, smiling, those gold flecks she'd noticed in his eyes sparkling. But now, his expression sobered, his lips no longer turned upward, but set in a serious line. His intense stare sent a shiver over her skin.

As she approached speaking distance, she found her pulse racing even as her pace slowed. Finally, she came to a halt in front of him and drank in the sight of the man—boots, jeans, T-shirt, flannel. Handsome features, and that hair she suspected he'd never admit he'd started wearing long expressly because his household of girls enjoying playing beauty salon. Lynnie and Molly had told her that ages ago, when Sloane was still mooning at him through her windows whenever she got the chance, her crush in the seedling stage.

What a shallow emotion it was compared to that deep well he'd carved in her heart now.

"Eli—"

"Sloane—"

They both spoke at once.

Not trusting her suddenly rusty voice, she gestured him to go ahead.

He stared at her another long minute. "Sloane, you look…" He laughed a little, the sound rough. Then he shook his head, the gesture rueful. "Right. You look right."

"Oh." Without knowing what to make of that, she took a small step forward. "Let me take Paige."

"No." He drew the little girl closer to his chest. "She feels exactly right too—just where she is."

"Oh," Sloane said again, nonplused.

"I'm sorry I didn't get it before," Eli said. "I didn't get it until just now, as you were walking to me while I had Paige in my arms."

She swallowed. "Get what?"

His gaze didn't leave hers. "I'm in love with you, Sloane."

Suddenly unbalanced, she stumbled back, trying to find stability in a world suddenly rocking.

"I think it happened that night during the storm, when you knocked on the front door and I opened it to find all of you drenched and shivering. You walked into my house and you walked into my heart." With Paige hitched on his hip, one arm providing a sturdy seat for her behind, he had a free hand that he scrubbed over his face. "I've fallen in love," he said, a note of wonder in his voice.

Then he laughed again. "Much better than an excellent turf builder."

"What?"

He laughed some more. "Can I explain later? After I say or do whatever it will take to get you over here next to me?"

Sloane was having a hard time breathing. And believing. "Why would you fall in love with the last person you should want?"

"Because *I* need rescuing," he said without hesitation. "You and Paige are going to rescue me from something that's all wrong for me."

Those sounded like magic words, but she'd not gotten this far in a life that too often presented obstacles to throw caution to the wind now. "What's that mean exactly?"

"I thought I wanted simplicity. A stress-free life." Eli shrugged. "But it turns out I'm a family man...to the bone. It took only a few hours in a silent house for me to realize I'm happiest smack-dab in the middle of chaos and laughter and, most of all, love."

*Oh, wow.*

In the distance, someone shouted Paige's name and the little girl wiggled in Eli's grasp. He set her down and she ran off. Over her shoulder, Sloane saw the man's twin sisters each take one of her daughter's hands. They were smiling, bright as the sun beaming down like a benediction.

Like a blessing she'd only felt once before, on the day that Paige was born.

"Eli," she said. *He loved her?* "Can...can this be true?"

He held out his arms. "Come here and find out."

Sloane did, taking a chance that suddenly didn't feel like a chance at all. As Eli had said, it just felt...right.

His embrace was warm, his kiss deep, the unspoken words traded between them filled her soul. He lifted his head to stare into her eyes. "Anything else concerning you?"

Her lips twitched. "What about Baby Sally? She comes with the package."

"I told you, I'm over my fear."

"Liar."

He smiled, and touched his forehead to hers. "No. And maybe there'll be other babies someday."

The final gate of her heart opened, and the very last vestiges of caution and fear poured out. Closing her eyes, she buried her face in his chest. Eli allowed that for a few moments, then he slipped a finger under her chin to bring her gaze back to his.

His features swam in her vision. "I've been alone for so long," she said. "All my life. When I left you yesterday, I thought it would be easy to be alone again."

"I thought I *wanted* to be alone…that I'd tapped out my capacity for caring," Eli said. "That was, as you pointed out, just an excuse."

"I sound so wise," she said, smiling at him.

"You were. You are. I want you and I want Paige in my life, more than anything. Because as it turns out, when it comes to love there's no limit."

Tears burned in her eyes again, then finally spilled over. "Here's a thing you don't know about me," she said, wet trails running down her cheeks. "I never cry."

"Except with me," he whispered, reminding her of another time, when she'd been overcome by passion. "Except in my arms. And I swear you'll always be safe there, and cherished."

Her first, last, and forever wish, Sloane thought, she who had given up believing in such things for herself so long ago. "I'm going to make you happy," she promised.

"No doubt, no limits." He smiled. "Carpe diem."

"Yes," she whispered. "We'll do that. Seize the day. It's a fine way to live a fine life."

Eli's next kiss expressed that he fully agreed.


## THE END

# About The Author

Christie Ridgway is the author of over sixty novels of contemporary romance. All her books are both sexy and emotional and tell about heroes and heroines who learn to believe in the power of love. A *USA Today* bestseller, Christie is a six-time RITA finalist and has won best contemporary romance of the year and career achievement awards from *Romantic Times Book Reviews*.

A native of California, Christie now resides in the southern part of the state with her family. Inspired by the beaches, mountains, and cities that surround her, she writes tales of sunny days and steamy nights. For a complete list of books, excerpts, and news on the latest going on with Christie:

*Visit Christie's Website*:
www. christieridgway.net

*Join Christie on Facebook:*
www.facebook.com/christieridgway

*Follow Christie on Twitter:*
http://www.twitter.com/christieridgway

Made in the USA
San Bernardino, CA
03 June 2019